Protecting Delaina

A Dark Hitman Romantic Suspense

by

CJ Warrant

It's like *kill or be killed*, that's my thing basically.

— Lucy Liu

Merrick's Rules

There's only two rules to follow. Never regret pulling the trigger. And never kill the innocent. Falling in love isn't one of them.

Merrick Gentry has two jobs, complete the contract and collect the money. He also has two rules. Never regret pulling the trigger, and never kill an innocent. But the moment he scopes out Delaina Wells, his spotless career as a hitman implodes and chaos ensues.

As more killers come out of the woodwork, Merrick eliminates anyone that threatens her life. Keeping her safe and alive is his goal. Not fall hard for the dark-haired beauty with a sassy mouth.

When there's a million dollars on the line for her life, Delaina Wells isn't sure who to turn to. Yet, she has no choice but to trust the gorgeous hitman she attracted to, or die in the hands of other killers, who wants to cash in the prize.

From killer to protector, Merrick's abilities are put through the ringer, and so is his heart when his desire for Delaina could get them both killed. He needs his guard up and find who took out the hit, or they both will be six feet under.

1

Merrick

UNDER THE INTENSE August heat of the Florida sun, I lie still beneath the old mangrove roots on the west side of the property where my mark resides. My legs are partially submerged in swamp water, surrounded by an ecosystem that can swim up and bite me in the ass and suck me under until I'm primed for eating.

All of this, for a cool mil. Is it worth it? Yes... or so I thought until I saw my mark.

"The money is too good to pass up, Merrick," Joe, my handler, insisted to me a few weeks ago before I relented and accepted the job. I want to beat the shit out of him at times for picking up contracts that put my life in a precarious place. Like this fucking swamp filled with gators.

The money will be worthless to me if I'm dead.

I shove that thought aside and focus on the mobile home in my line of sight. When I first arrived on this God forsaken inlet, I thought I'd finish the job within the day. But I immediately had reservations on pulling the trigger. My gut told me to hold off. The niggling suspicion that keeps pounding louder in my head hasn't relented with each passing hour either.

Why? I simply don't know.

I have no problem taking out garbage from this world. With a single bullet from my *Katie,* a CheyTac M200 with an NXS scope, they forfeit their lives for the shitty things they've done in this world. *If* they deserve it. And normally they do. Then I slink my sorry ass back to my tiny unencumbered town in the northern part of Vermont with the easy cash in my account.

However, this mark's different. She's a woman—which I don't have an issue killing—if she deserves it. But I've been watching Delaina Wells for a full week. She's no scum of the earth like my usual marks. She has no outrageous wealth displayed. Hell, the 1985 beige Subaru Outback she drives is band-aided together with silver duct tape on the front and back bumpers. I can guarantee that vehicle has way more miles on its four-cylinder engine than most old clunkers on the road.

She parks that piece of shit at the airpark across the waterway and every day drives it to the café she works at in Everglade City. Then she takes the outboard skiff that's tied to the tiny pier to this ten-acre property, where her single-wide sits like a rusted out open sore.

Delaina's no beauty queen. And what I mean by that is

there's no vanity shown in her. By clothing or jewelry, or the minimal makeup regimen she undergoes on the daily. There haven't been any extravagant shopping trips or expensive salon visits. Her light brown, curly hair is always up in a messy bun on top of her head, except when a few tendrils get free and frame her oval face. Then my fingers twitch, and I want to walk up to her and sweep them around her ears, to see if her hair feels as soft as it appears to be.

Simple is what I would call her. And breathtaking.

Her rich espresso eyes might be called hypnotic, but the smattering of freckles across the bridge of her straight nose is damn distracting.

Delaina's just shy of five-six, with long, attractive legs. Her bronzed skin is reminiscent of smooth expensive silk, which has me thinking all too much of touching her in ways I shouldn't be thinking about my mark.

I quickly bury that frisson of want deep down where no thoughts grow and remain eye contact through my scope.

The woman lives paycheck to paycheck, with barely a hundred dollars in her savings account. When I say Delaina Wells is no one special to pay attention to, more ordinary than most, I'm talking truth. She isn't the typical garbage I focus down the barrel for. Not a scumbag at all.

Then why does someone want her dead?

That question is on repeat in my head, but I come up with nothing.

I pull just a hair back when a glint of silver catches my

peripheral to the left. I freeze, and slowly—very slowly, turn my head a few millimeters in that direction.

There. Against a Florida pine, I see it—or should I say, him... or her. Where hitmen are concerned, there's no discrimination on the genders.

Damn it. An overwhelming need to protect Delaina rushes at me like a three-hundred-pound linebacker. Besides, I got here first.

As to whoever is hiding in the underbrush across the way, I decide to change my tactics and see who's after my mark. With a million on the line, there's no doubt this killer is here to take out Delaina and collect the big cash prize.

Leaving my Katie on point, I silently slither deeper into the swamp water until my nostrils skim above the waterline. I cringe at the rotten egg stench of the Everglades. But what do you expect from the combination of wet earth, decaying vegetation, and stagnant saltwater surrounding me.

Staying near the edge of the bank, I slowly creep forward but remain alert for nearby gators, cottonmouths, or eastern corals.

With my KA-BAR knife in hand, I glide silently to that side of the property. Not ten feet away, there're legs camouflaged by fabricated grasses, dirt, and pine branches. If I want to surprise this fucker, I have to be quick.

Cautiously I move closer. Five feet away now. I'm about to leap out of the water when Delaina's loud skiff chuffs up to the small rickety dock that is on its last pillar.

Shit. She's home early.

I have to take down this hitter before he reacts and

pulls the trigger, and Delaina ends up with a bullet in her head.

A slight shift disturbs a pine branch that's stacked on top of the human mound. Before Delaina reaches the mobile home, I don't hesitate and launch at the sneaky fucker. But the assassin knew where I was, too, and quickly twists his upper torso, pointing the 9 mm right at my face.

I swiftly knock the guy's Ruger out of his hold, slice at his wrist and immediately turn him on his back. He grunts in pain while trying to wrestle out of my grasp, but I draw my knife under his chin, barely cutting into the flesh next to his jugular.

With my knees locking down his arms, blood pooling from his lacerated wrist, I lean in and put a finger to my lips to tell him to stay quiet.

I take this moment to memorize his pocked face. Bald, a bit on the rangy side. His light blue eyes are cold, calculating, and emotionless. Like mine.

He doesn't move, not even his eyes, which are trained on my face and boring through me like honed ice picks. Considering his Winchester Magnum is pointed toward Delaina's place, the implication of who this man is and why he's here rings true to my earlier scenario. He's here to take out *my* mark.

The sound of keys rattling perks my ears, but my eyes remain coldly faceted on the killer under me. Then the front door of Delaina's trailer slams shut. It must not be a good day for her either.

Knowing I'm in the clear, I lean in almost nose to nose and demand, "Who the fuck are you?" Nothing but chill comes off his silent demeanor. So, I repeat myself, as I tuck the knife tighter against his neck until a thin line of blood forms on the blade's edge. "Who the fuck are you?"

"Why are you on my mark?" he counters evenly, as though we're having a casual conversation.

"Last time, buddy." I know this is a useless question, but I have to try. "Who hired you to be on *my* mark?"

"You know how this game goes, Merrick Gentry. Now, either kill me or get the fuck off of me."

How in the hell does he know my name?

I know I've made a name in this business, but no one knows my face... Until now.

I don't go sharing my shit worldwide. So this is a problem.

I study his face a bit more. There's a slight sheen of perspiration across his furrowed brows. In his steady gaze there's a knowing that he's a dead man, no matter what he says. Hell, I wouldn't either if I was in his shoes. But I'm better than him.

I tighten my hold on the knife, the edge of the blade cutting deeper into his flesh. "How do you know me?" I emphasize with open hostility.

A smirk mixed with pain shadows across his face. "Everyone knows who you are now, Merrick. And as for your previous question, I'm here for the same reason as you are. One. Million. Dollars."

His words have my body locking even tighter than Aunt Winnie's pickle jar.

"Everyone knows who I am." What, the, fuck?

It's dawning on me that someone has two hitters for one slip of a woman. Why?

Now there's no way I'm killing Delaina Wells—not until I get to the bottom of this shit.

For a second, my mind drifts and the asshole takes advantage. His right arm slips free from under my left knee, and the sneaky bastard slams a small dagger he pulled out of nowhere and the short blade cuts into the outer edge of my thigh. The knife might be small, but it's lethal and sharp.

Thankfully, it didn't hit my femoral artery, which this asshole was probably aiming for.

I snap my teeth closed and quietly hiss, "Fuck." Blood seeps through my slashed cargos, but I can't worry about it right now.

I bite back a growl as he pulls the blade out and tries to jab at my face, but I don't hesitate and slice my fat blade across his throat. He lets out a strangled gasp as blood gushes out of his carotid. My hand covers his gaping mouth as he gurgles out his last breath. The blue of his eyes loses its intensity and the panic fades into stillness.

Fuck. Fuckity-fuck!

I didn't want to kill him just yet. I have more questions about who hired him and what he meant by everyone knowing who I am now. But he left me with no choice.

This isn't what I expected today. But in this line of work, one has to anticipate the unexpected. Even another hitman coming at you.

I take in a heavy breath and release it, centering myself before digging into the killer's pockets.

Finding a receipt time-stamped seven-ten yesterday morning from the restaurant where Delaina works, my gut twists at the idea that he knew I was already here. Honestly, I'm surprised he didn't take me out firsthand before aiming his barrel at Delaina. His loss.

There's a hiss and a splash behind me. I turn, eyeing movements in the water. I quickly check the rest of the dead man's pockets, finding nothing else—not even a wallet. Then I pull his lifeless body into the water.

"Gator bait," I say with a smile.

Once the body is submerged, I ease back to my place under the mangrove tree. After checking my wound, I dry the area and superglue the small one-inch gash. Then I turn my attention back to the trailer, but this time I keep my legs out of the water.

With solid ground under me, I hear loud crashes coming from inside the trailer. I'm instantly on alert. Looking through the scope, the dirty, screened windows show nothing but closed blinds.

Right then, Delaina stumbles out of the trailer with a bottle of tequila in hand and plops her shapely ass down on the small wooden porch and starts bawling. I see her lips moving with soundless words. Between the tears falling from her eyes and the agony across her—bruised face?

"Now where the fuck did you get those bruises?" I whisper, knowing her face was unmarred when she left this morning.

She continues talking and crying to herself, having a full blown argument with no one. My heart speeds up and my gut knots at seeing her distressed. There's no fucking way I can ever put a bullet in her. She is one of the innocents I promised myself a long time ago I would never kill, for any amount of money.

After a guttural scream, Delaina guzzles back what's left of the alcohol in the bottle and then chucks the glass container against the rusted metal shed before stalking back inside and slamming the door.

In the week I've been observing her, not once did she show any rage or displeasure. Until today.

Someone has put those bruises on Delaina's face and has her so angry that she turns to alcohol. I want to know who. And I want to know now.

There's only one person who can give me those answers. I pull out my phone and call Joe.

This is his deal. Joe should be able to scratch up more information about Delaina's life and why she's so important that someone wants her dead, and hires two hitmen. Who could have laid their hand on her? And how did the other hitman know who I am?

"Job done already?" Joe briskly answers the phone, surprise edging his voice.

"Did you send another hitter to my mark?" Silence. "Joe? Do I need to track you down and put the hurt on your sorry ass?"

"No—"

"Don't fucking lie to me, asshole," I warn, turning toward the waters and watching a white egret take flight. The bird has a tranquil bearing, which reminds me of Delaina. But I bet underneath her beauty, there's a wild side. And I just saw a glimpse of it.

"I'm not. Why would I do a stupid thing like that?" Joe admits with a hesitation.

"Because I took one out not ten minutes ago," I say with clenched teeth. "He also said that everyone knows who I am. What the fuck does that mean, Joe? What did you get me into?"

A rush of clicks echoes from the other end of the phone. "Hold on—Shit. Did the hitter actually say that?"

"Yes," I spit out.

"Okay—okay. Give me a second." He mumbles through the clicks and clacks, while I impatiently lay there under the shade, my eyes trained on the now-quiet trailer.

After a several long minutes, my tolerance is worn so thin, it's clear as glass. "Well?"

"The client that took out the contract hired three more hitters. The latest one just five minutes ago."

What the fuck? Three? Four including me.

"How's this possible?" I utter, more to myself than to Joe.

"Whoever wants her dead has to be desperate," Joe says with more clicks on his end. "But the job is done, right?"

I snort. "No."

"What? Why?"

"Did you get any leads why my name is out there?" I growl out, completely ignoring his question.

"No, not yet. But, dude, what are you waiting for? Finish the contract." There's a hint of desperation in his voice, which isn't like Joe at all. Granted, there have been times that he's opened his mouth before thinking, but that's due to over imbibing in too much caffeine. Or he hasn't slept for more than two days. But I don't think this is one of those times.

"Something is off," I finally admit, glancing down at the screen.

"Shit, Merrick. This isn't the time to think. Tell me she'll be dead by the end of today and we could walk away with the million."

The greedy motherfucker.

"I want to know what's so important about this girl, and who in Delaina Wells's life would put their hands on her. I also want to know who's spreading my name and face around. Got me, Joe?" I demand with rising annoyance, ignoring his whiny plea.

He expels a hitched breath. "Fine," he drags out. "If there's more to this girl, I'll find it."

Joe's the best damn hacker around. That's one reason why he's my handler, aside from a few other qualities about the money grubbing bastard.

"I want everything as soon as you get it. Understand?" I glance back at the trailer. "Look into the property, too. It bumps up against the Everglades. It might be worth something, if someone thinks it's worth killing for."

"Nothing's different from what I emailed you last week."

"I don't want a fucking recap, Joe. Give me something new," I growl into the phone.

"You're not going to kill her, are you?" A curbed irritation settles in his tone.

"Joe," I bark, but it's too late, the asshole hung up. I

glare down at my phone before tucking it back into my pocket. I hate it when he hangs up on me. It's a pet peeve I can't stand, and Joe does it all the fucking time. On purpose.

I don't give two shits if Joe's pissed off. Money isn't as important to me as it is to him. I don't kill the innocent, and this mark is innocent. I can feel it down to my bones that I'm right.

As for Delaina's background, which is basic and easy to remember. Her stepfather, Brent Miller, owns three car dealerships. One in Sarasota, another in Miami, and one in Orlando. And her stepbrother, Mark is the sales manager for the Orlando branch. There is no blood family living.

She's alone.

But there's more than meets the eye with Delaina Wells. And if I'm going to find out, I will need to get close to her. With a million up for grabs, my concern at this point is the other hitmen coming for her. Tomorrow, with Treg's help, I will uncover who my mark really is.

2

Delaina

THROUGH THE PARTIALLY OPEN blinds of my bedroom window, the light from the rising sun cuts into my alcohol-induced sleep. I have no choice but to open my eyes, and then wince.

Without having to look at the alarm clock on the night-stand, I know it's almost seven in the morning.

"Go to hell, Monday," I mumble against my pillow, roll over, and try to go back to sleep. But my face hurts and so I roll onto my back. I lay there all of thirty seconds before one eye pops open. Tilting my head to the left, I spot an empty bottle of Wild Turkey sitting on the other night-stand, blatantly jeering back at me. This isn't a good start to my day.

A drunken night with tequila and a half a bottle of

whiskey leaves me with a heavy dose of resentment and a killer headache that'll probably stick with me into tomorrow.

As much as I want to get up, do my normal routine of showering and getting ready for work, this morning I won't be doing any of that. Instead, I'll get up, make a pot of coffee, and look for another job. And hopefully, Mark won't find out where that new job is.

I close my eyes for a long moment and attempt to not let what happened yesterday ruin today. However, I'm openly raw, like the pain radiating from my jaw from the punch my stepbrother delivered to me.

I don't know why he showed up at the diner. Out of all the times he has tormented me over the years, yesterday took the cake. Mark has caused so much trouble for me in the past, but now I've lost my job because of that asshole. I'm just grateful I got away before he did something worse.

No matter how much I try not to cry, I can't forget the malicious attack or the degrading words that cut deeper than the sharpest blade.

The saddest part of all is that my boss saw the whole diabolical assault unfold and the bastard did nothing to stop it.

I was so shaken up from the attack that I even spilled hot coffee on poor Miss Maddy's sweater. At least I didn't scald her tender old flesh. That would hurt me more than losing any job or getting assaulted by my stepbrother. In the end, it didn't matter what I did or said. I was fired for *almost* burning the woman.

"Fuck!" I abruptly scream at the top of my lungs, tears

leaking from the corners of my eyes and my entire body shaking with so much pent-up anger. "Why, damnit? Why?"

"No more tears, Delaina. I promise it will be all better tomorrow." I can hear my mother's supportive words trying to soothe me. "Right, Mom. It's already tomorrow and it's not any better."

I ruefully chuckle into the quiet of the bedroom. Even though my emotions are nothing but brittle and broken, I have no choice but to shake off the dark mood and keep moving.

I get out of bed while avoiding the long mirror on the closet door. There's no doubt bruises shadow my cheek and jaw; I just don't want a visual reminder.

Halfway to the kitchen, my foot catches on the loose thread-bare carpet, and I nearly careen face-first into the wall. But I quickly right myself. I look down and my big toe is snared in green and red carpet threads.

All I want to do is throw shit around and scream again. Why do I even bother staying here? I can go anywhere—be in some other town—in another state—doing something I love, like being a nurse.

I don't have to deal with all this shit. Being bullied by family. Or getting blindsided and attacked while taking out the garbage.

But here I am, until my twenty-seventh birthday. I made a promise to my grandparents. A promise I can't go back on.

Besides, with my birthday barreling in at the end of the month, the oath I gave myself three years ago—to have enough money to get out, is a total fail. It may take me another year, but I'm bound and determined to be far away from Florida and away from Mark.

I never understood why I had to stay on this land. It's only ten acres—and most of the property is Everglades.

Guiltily, I tried to sell it once. I even asked my stepfather Brent to help me put it up for sale. But he told me no one wants this God forsaken land. He says it's a useless piece of property and I should give it away.

My grandparents entrusted me with these ten acres until I see fit to sell it to the right buyer on the year of my twenty-seventh birthday. And I haven't met one yet who wants or is worthy of land.

A couple months back, Brent suggested he'd take the land off my hands for a few thousand, but I know this place is worth more than the pennies he has offered me, and I told him no. Needless to say, he wasn't happy with my answer, but too damn bad.

Desperate for caffeine, I reach the kitchen and almost step on the broken plates, coffee cups and shards of glass that are scattered across the linoleum floor. The living room is no better.

"What a mess." *Just like my damn life.*

Luckily, I didn't break every dish and cup in the cabinets, but enough to fill the garbage can.

After I start the pot of coffee, I pick up the large pieces, sweep the floor and toss everything into the garbage pail. As I heft up the can and walk to the front door, a strange scratching noise comes from the back door.

I lower the can and slowly reach for the wooden bat

that once belonged to my biological father, who was a huge Red Sox fan. Sometimes I wonder—if he hadn't died in a training accident, would my life be different?

"Wishing is like a dream, Delaina. You can see it, but it'll never be fulfilled. Unless you do something about it." It's the last thing my mother told me before she left for work that morning. She died later that afternoon in car accident.

I carefully cross the floor, making sure my feet avoid the areas where there's creaking. Just past the tiny bistro table, I lean against the refrigerator and cautiously peek out the back door. Through the glass, I see nothing but the water and trees, the brightness of the rising sun and the clear cut of the blushing sky.

I lower my bat an inch when the scratching resumes. With the weapon gripped tight in my hand again, I press my face to the window and finally look down. There, on the small back stoop, is a medium-size dog, all muddy and totally unrecognizable in breed. I can't tell what color it is from the amount of sludge on the animal's fur.

The dog angles his head up, tongue out and panting. His eyes are mixed, one blue and one brown. A warmth of excitement and elation hits me as I stare down at the animal. I wanted a pet when I was a child, but always got denied.

With a quick look around, I put the bat down on the counter and cautiously open the door. To my surprise, the dog drops down on its haunches, his tiny tail wagging furiously as though the animal's happy to see me.

I drop to my knees, eye level with the dog. "Where did

you come from, boy—if you're an actual boy. What's your name, sweetheart?" I coo, like the dog would answer back, and slowly extend a hand.

You're an idiot, Delaina.

I hold my breath for a moment as the dog sniffs my fingers. A cold, wet nose meets my warm palm and a second or two later, I have a slimy, sludge-coated animal in my arms. Licks of his rough tongue on my face have me giggling like a school girl.

"Who do you belong to?" I ask, looking around the yard to see if there's any evidence of the dog's owner, but nobody is around. I glance back down at the dog and smile. "I guess I should clean you up to see what you really look like. Then maybe under all that muck and matted fur, there's a collar."

I get up from the floor, carrying the muddy furball to the bathroom.

Not thinking twice, I climb into the tub with the dog and turn on the water. It takes three shampoos to get all the mud and grime off the animal's coat. He has a collar, but sadly no tags. At least I know he is a he, which I found out while cleaning his underbelly.

He's a small collie of some sort. A handsome looking animal, with patches of gray and black against his white coat.

After washing him up, I get out and let him shake off his fur in the tub. Everything got wet—including me, and I don't mind. It's nothing but a quick wipe down of the tub won't fix. For me, I head to the bedroom for a quick change of clothes, the wet dog following closely behind.

Eyeing the pile of dirty clothes on the floor, knowing I have to go the laundromat, I forgo a bra and undies, and change into a dirty t-shirt and shorts until I've had a shower.

It's not like anyone is going to stare at my boobs.

"Are you hungry, dog?" I smile down at the animal. I can't keep calling him dog... "What should I call you?"

He barks and I can't help but laugh.

I study his face and come up with... "You look like a Luke. How about that?"

Luke barks again, and spins in a quick circle.

"I guess you approve."

My bruised face hurts from grinning, but it feels good to let loose those emotions. Geez, I can't remember the last time I was truly happy. I'll keep calling him Luke until I find his owner. Unless I end up keeping him.

You can't afford a dog.

Sometimes I want to slap my conscience.

As Luke follows me to the kitchen, my stomach growls. I chuckle at the absurdity of the sound coming from my body. Since I only had a liquid meal last night, it's no wonder my insides are making noise. "Guess I'll join you."

I lay a dry towel down on the floor for Luke and then scan the meager contents of the fridge, pulling out the pizza box from two nights ago. "I think coffee and pizza will do for me. Do you want a slice?"

Luke yips and sits up on his haunches, one forepaw up. He did it with ease, like he's been practicing that move for a long while. Whoever trained him, knew what he was doing.

I eye Luke, before putting a slice of pizza on a plate and placing it in front of him. "Don't eat too fast."

With the coffee ready, I'm pulling one of the last two remaining mugs from the cabinet when a knock at the front door draws me up short. I automatically reach for the bat.

I glance down at the dog, who sits patiently by my feet, pizza not touched. "Can it be your owner?" I hope not, but I quickly banish that thought.

As I cautiously head for the front door, another thought slams into my brain. *Please, don't let it be Mark.*

But he wouldn't knock. The bastard would kick down the door instead and barrel inside. So no, it can't be him. That leaves only one conclusion. It has to be Luke's—no, the dog's owner.

With another glance down at Luke, I take those tentative steps and peer through the peephole. My head rears back immediately and I lose all the air in my lungs as a pair of stormy blue-gray eyes peers back at the door. My heart kicks up speed, giving me a rush of adrenalin, I'm not used to feeling when looking a man. A gorgeous man to boot.

Damn. I quickly look through the peephole again, and this time, I see a broad chest, rugged shoulders, and muscled arms that can probably carry the world. The man on the other side of the door is pure perfection. But his frown is... intimidating, like he lost his... "Luke."

While I take a moment to gather myself, he knocks hard on the door.

I take an unsteady breath, shaking off the endorphins pinging through my system, and then casually open the door part way. "Can I help... you?" I stumble out the greeting, forcing my lips into a small shaky smile.

Keep smiling, damn it.

"I'm sorry to bother you, but..." His attention swiftly roams my bruised face before recentering back onto my eyes.

Shit. I totally forgot about my face. Now what does he think of me? I want to slam the door and hide from him, but instead, I straighten my spine, while my stomach's churning. "Yes?"

"Can you tell me if you've seen a dog around here?"

"What kind?" I ask, shifting my gaze to the top of his head—away from his intrusive stare. Like I'm in some frickin' trance, I forget my embarrassment of the bruises, and slowly peruse the man like he's standing there, all for me to gawk at.

"He's an Australian Collie mix, with a black, gray, and white coat. He also has two different colored eyes."

I hear him talking, but my brain is too focused on how the man is a good five inches taller than me. And then my eyes drop to his light moss-colored Henley stretched tight, which suggests well-defined pectorals. Not able to help myself, my focus drop down to where the shirt is tucked into his black cargo shorts, then back up to his face.

"Ma'am?"

"What?" I finally meet his eyes.

"The dog," he mumbles out through clenched teeth.

"The dog. The dog?" *Oh, God, I sound like an idiot.*

"Are you alright?"

My cheeks instantly flush hot the moment I feel his

strong hand on my arm. Every inch of my skin prickles with electricity from his touch. I want to pull away, but at the same time climb him like a tree.

Instead of answering him like a normal human being, I stare at his brownish-blond hair trailing his collar. I so badly want to run my fingers through the thick strands, as well as the scruff highlighting his square jawline. I wonder what it would feel like against my—

Good God. Get a grip!

I clear my throat. "Sorry. Haven't had my morning coffee yet. Now about your dog."

A slip of a smile crests his lips, and I want to swoon like a lovesick fool. But I shut that crap down and stoically say, "How did your dog get lost out here? It's hard getting to this side of the property, especially when the river and Glades surround three sides. There's only one way in and out."

Apprehension suddenly shoots through the roof at the realization that no—I mean hardly ever anyone drives or walks here, unless they have reason. I grip the bat tighter and study this man's face with renewed focus.

"I got lost on the main road yesterday and found your driveway to turn around in, but Treg jumped out of the window and chased after a heron. I tried going after him, but he disappeared from my sight and I've been looking for him ever since," he says coolly, his eyes never leaving my face, which I find unnerving and uncomfortable.

Crap. He's staring at my bruises.

I want to hide my face, step back, and close the door, but I'm caught in his mesmerizing eyes. This close, they are more blue than gray. Stark and intense, and never wavering.

Nervously shifting my feet, I drop my eyes to the chunky expensive watch on his left wrist. It's one I'm not familiar with, but I guarantee the price is up there. Granted, I can't judge the man's words by the watch he's wearing, but why would he lie?

And if what he said is true, then his explanation is plausible. With the narrow, one-car drive through the property, he would have no choice but to turn around by the trailer. And he's right. There are tons of herons around here for Lu—no, Treg to chase after.

As my apprehension slides back a little, I straighten my shoulders and open the door fully. "Yes. I actually found your dog earlier this morning. He must have been in the edge of the marshy wetlands because he was all mucked up when he landed on my stoop." I open the screen door and look back at the dog stationed by the fridge.

The man drops to his knees and lets out a shrill whistle. "Tregus."

A mound of fluff rushes past me and into the man's arms, butt wiggling and his tongue offering face licks. I'm suddenly jealous of the amount of attention the dog is getting from this man. Or vice versa.

And what's with the stupid name? I like Luke much better, but I keep that to myself.

"Tregus? That's a strange name for a dog." *Rude, De.*

He looks up from his dog's adoration, his sparkling eyes hitting me in the stomach like a battering ram, and a riot of butterflies takes flight. I quickly swallow down the shot of lust wetting my shorts and concentrate on the pair.

"Yes. He came with the name. But I mostly call him Treg for short." A tiny mischievous grin tips his lips. "The name suits him."

I still like Luke better.

I quickly look away before an ounce of my desire shows on my face and I do something utterly idiotic like jump into the man's arms and ask him to pet me. *God, De. Desperate much?*

I cross and uncross my arms. "You know you should get tags for him. Who knows, next time he might not be so lucky to find someone like me."

"Treg has one, but the damn dog keeps chewing it off," he says with a soft chuckle. He stands and extends a hand. "I'm Mike Gent." My eyes drop to said large hand and I gulp down a whimper.

I'm so into large hands on a guy. His knuckles are scabbed and there're callouses on his palm. Hmm. Working man's hands. *Nice.*

Jesus, I can't seem to control the desire pulsing through my veins every time I stare at the man.

A loud snort escapes out of me when his hand encapsulates mine, and I promptly pull away, covering my mouth in mortification. "I'm sorry. I don't know where that came from."

"That's okay," he admits easily, like people snort like a pig around him all the time.

"Sorry." I clear my throat. "Well, it's nice to meet you. Here's your *clean* dog."

"Thanks for washing Treg up and taking care of him." He steps off the stoop, calling the dog to his side.

I notice Mike's slight limp, which has my eyes detouring straight to his fine round ass. *Oh my.*

"Don't let that man leave." The odd demand pops into my head like a warning bell.

I don't know what's wrong with me. I never let strangers in my house, but before I can think twice, I call out, "Did you get injured? I can take a look at it if you want. I'm a trained nurse." The lie comes out easy. He doesn't need to know the amount of medical knowledge I have... or don't have.

Mike pauses mid-step, before calling over his shoulder, "Don't worry about it. It's only a graze." He continues walking.

"Well, too late. I'm already worried," I call back.

He stops, partially turns, and eyes me intently for a moment like he's contemplating his next move. "You don't know me, or what happened to my leg."

"It doesn't matter. My mother taught me to help people in need. And you look like you're in need." *Jesus, De. Now you sound like a bigger idiot than before.*

"What do you think?" He looks down at Treg, brushing his hand over the dog's head.

"I have coffee?" *Like that's going to woo him to drop his shorts.*

Mike tilts his sculpted jaw skyward like he's checking the sun. Then he does the strangest thing. He scans the property before he utters, "Sure."

I release a puff of breath before stepping back into the

trailer. "He said yes," I utter under my breath as nervous energy jolts through me.

What is going on? I never invite people—let alone a guy, inside my place for anything. Not coffee or to check his injury. Am I that desperate—just so I can see his butt—no. I'm better than that... I think.

I scan the living room and kitchen, making sure I picked up all the debris from my tirade yesterday. Satisfied with the cleanup, I make sure the coffee pot is full and then head to the bathroom for the first aid kit from the cabinet under the sink.

With a quick look in the mirror, I grimace at the state I'm in. The bruise is larger than what I thought. And I look more like a deranged raccoon than a human being. The dark circles around my eyes are from lack of sleep, intoxication, and yesterday's makeup I didn't wash off. And let's not forget the ratted beehive of a mess on top of my head. I'm a total train wreck.

I grab the washcloth from the sink, wet it, and attempt to rub around my eyes to remove the smeared black eyeliner and mascara, but it's pointless. Then for a second, I am tempted to reach for my cover up to hide the purplish-yellow bruise across my jaw and cheek, or my split lip. But what's the point? Mike has already seen the state I'm in.

I drop the washcloth in the sink and am heading out of the bathroom when, out of the corner of my eye, I spot Mike stepping inside the trailer, with Treg right on his heels. Before he closes the door, he takes a long look around the property. *So strange.*

The muscles running along his neck and jaw tense,

and I wonder what he's worried about. His eyes narrow, focusing on the line of mangrove trees lining the water's edge.

"Is everything all right?" I ask, stepping next to him and glancing in the same general direction he was looking, but I don't see anything unusual.

Mike's entire body tenses up before his face softens, his stance relaxes, and he chuckles, "Sorry about that. I'm just thinking that Treg is a very lucky dog that a gator didn't get him."

I relax. "Yeah. If I had a dog, I would be worried about that, too." I don't know why, but I get the feeling he's holding something back. Or it's the alcohol from last night's over-imbibing that might have discombobulated my brain and I can't tell right from left.

Mike closes the door, turns, and scans my home like he did to the mangroves.

"It ain't much, but it's rent free," I admit, chewing on my lower lip.

"It's a nice place." Mike studies my wall of meager pictures by the door.

I snort again, and promptly cover my mouth. "Umm... Thanks, but you don't have to lie. This rundown trailer and property used to belong to my grandparents. When they died, this paradise became all mine." There's no hiding the snark and irritation of my circumstance. I usually keep my baggage to myself. But here I am, telling a virtual stranger about my life. Or part of it.

"I'm sorry." He frowns at me.

Apparently, he doesn't get my sarcasm. "Sorry for what? My grandparents' deaths or this place?"

"Both, I guess. You don't sound happy." He goes back to studying the photos of my family. "Losing people you love is hard."

I want to laugh at his remark and his blindness to what's around him. If I'd known inviting this person into my home would start a discussion of dead family and my feelings, I wouldn't have asked Mike inside. But he's right about one thing. Losing my grandparents—and my mom, was hard—still is, at times.

"Well, life is what it is." I don't want to sound complacent, but when you get beat down so many times, it gets harder and harder every time you hit low.

I place the first aid kit on the table and stay quiet. The less he knows about me, the better.

"These must be your parents. Are they around?" He points to the only picture I have of them together. They were barely eighteen then, and immensely in love with each other since grade school. Crazy, isn't it?

I wished on plenty of stars above to find the same intense love they had for each other. However, love like that isn't in those stars for me.

"They're passed away, too." I don't say anymore.

Neither does Mike, until he walks to the electric fireplace with a wooden mantle my grandmother had loved.

"You were a cute kid," he says, pointing to the picture of Mom and me. I was five then.

The other picture is of me and my dad when I was

born. And the last frame is of my grandparents, which so happens to be adjacent to their urns.

To a stranger, the display would appear more of a shrine—which it is, in some sense. But Mike doesn't need to know that.

"How about that injury?" I ask, trying to mask the loss building in my chest.

Mike stares at the photos for a long moment like they hold answers for him. For me? I suddenly feel like I'm standing there naked and exposed as he studies my family.

I shake off the odd feeling and walk to the coffee pot. "Have a seat. I'll get the coffee. And then I'll check your leg."

"Thank you." *So polite.* "How did you get that bruise on your face?" *Maybe not so polite.*

I pause, turning my face away before another lie comes out of my mouth. "I tripped." It's my go-to excuse whenever Mark puts his hands on me. Again, this man doesn't need to know my business.

"That must have been some trip," he says with a lack of conviction.

Yeah, I don't believe me either.

I ignore his inquiry and be the good hostess my grandmother taught me to be. I set out the two mugs, sugar, some Splenda packets for me, and the non-dairy creamer on a round tray. Then I pour the hot coffee in the cups and carry the tray to the small kitchen table.

Mike sits down, taking my favorite mug that an old waitress friend gave me for my birthday a few years back.

The saying on it goes: *A Waitress's worst best friends: Bunions, No-chip Manicures & Cheap People.*

"Cream and sugar?" I chirp.

"No, thank you. I take mine black."

I sit across from Mike and quickly fix up my cup. Chancing a glance his way, I catch him eyeing my face again and then my chest. Dropping my eyes down to my shirt, I gasp at the sight. I'm instantly mortified that my nipples are hard, and they are poking against the thin fabric of my tank top.

I promptly fold my arms across my chest, whisper, "Excuse me," and race out of the kitchen to my bedroom. I snag an old sweatshirt haphazardly sticking out of my drawer and quickly put it on.

I close my eyes for a second and ask, "Why me?" while trying to calm my breathing so I don't hyperventilate and pass out.

It seems like forever before I regain some composure. With my nipples no longer on display, I head back to the kitchen and find Mike hasn't moved.

We sit there in awkward silence a whole thirty seconds before I take a sip of coffee. "I hope you like your coffee strong," I say, not sure what to talk about.

He takes a sip and closes his eyes. "Umm... Good coffee," he says in a light hearted tone.

What was that? Humor?

Another snort ekes out of me. "I'm sorry. I don't know what's wrong with me this morning," I admit, shaking my head. "Lately, everything sounds funny."

One eyebrow hikes high, and his greyish-blue eyes

meet mine. "Maybe somebody's got your funny bone," he says dryly this time, while taking another sip.

"Umm... That's an old saying," I blurt out without thinking. If Mom or Grandma could see me now, they would chastise me for being rude.

"Something my... Yes, it is." He looks away from me while placing the cup down on the table.

I want him to finish his sentence. Who is he talking about? But I don't push. Instead, I turn the topic to his injury. "Now that we had our coffee, let me see your leg."

"I'm good. Really. It's just a scratch," he says, pulling my attention from the first aid kit to his rugged face.

"With you traipsing around these Everglades for your dog, who knows what type of infection you could get. Then what would Treg do if you got sick, or worse?" I eye him studiously, not backing down. Trickery works fine, especially when I get what I want. My mother used the guilt tactic with Brent. And it worked most of the time.

"Not necessary." His voice deepens slightly, which causes a light shiver to run down my spine before his words register, and my excitement bursts like a popped helium balloon.

"Fine. If you'd—"

Ping. Pop. Treg starts barking and suddenly I'm on my back with Mike on top of me. "Don't move," he growls in my face. Those two words have me freezing in place before he climbs off me and moves toward the front door with swift efficiency.

More pings and then a crash to my left has me swiveling my head in the direction of the family room. My heart drops at the sight of my grandparents' urns shattered in pieces and their dust billowing in the air.

"What the—" My words are cut off by the sight of a gun in Mike's hand.

Maybe inviting him in for coffee was a bad idea after all.

3

M errick

When the first bullet hit the back wall, my only thought was to save Delaina. If anyone is going to take her out, it's going to be me. But that won't happen. Unless... I don't finish that thought.

"Treg, down." I order my dog, who's barking at the door, to stop. He drops and goes quiet.

Fuck. I shouldn't have gone in for coffee, or stared at her perky tits, because my dick is a rigid pole in my pants, and my attention got diverted from the real problem. Another hidden sniper.

It takes me a moment to calculate where the bastard is hiding. I bet the hitter is in the same spot as the other piece of gator-bait I killed yesterday.

Another round of pings slices through the thin

aluminum siding of the mobile home. The bullets shatter the urns on the mantel, and the human dust clouds the room. A gasp of horror from Delaina has me looking over my shoulder.

She's lying on the ground in a fetal position, but her face—except for the bruising—is as white as fresh fallen snow in Vermont. Her wide eyes are filled with shock and tears as she stares at what remains of her family.

I want to go to her, but another shot through the window shatters the pane completely, leaving the space exposed and vulnerable. I draw my gun and move against the bookshelf. I'm just out of view of the big window.

There's only one way out of this shitstorm.

I drop and crawl to Delaina. She quickly tries to scramble away from me, but I catch her arm and put a halt to her escape. "I need you to go to your bedroom and hide in the closet. Hear me, Delaina? Don't leave the house or you're dead."

Her obsidian eyes go even wider with my threat, but I don't care. All I want is for her to stay alive and be safe.

She turns her head and doesn't say anything. Like avoiding my eyes will make this all go away. But she has another thing coming. I shake her slightly. "Do you understand me, Delaina? I want you to hide in the closet."

She frantically nods, tears streaking down her face now. "Okay."

"Take Treg with you. Stay low and lizard crawl to your room. You don't want a bullet in your pretty little brain." A gasp leaves her mouth, but I ignore her and turn to Treg. I give my dog a hand signal to follow Delaina and protect her. He whines, but he trails after her while she's on her stomach, clumsily sliding to the room. Once she closes the door, I move with speed.

Thank Christ, I checked out her place the first day I got here. I know every inch in this trailer—every escape route. The window in the second bedroom that faces the back half of the property is the best way out without being seen. I kick out the screen and slide myself through.

Once I've dropped into the tall grass that desperately needs mowing, I listen for more shots. All I hear are the grunts from the alligators and the slight chirps of the pig frogs.

Grateful for the obscurity provided by the overgrown junipers, honeysuckle, and ferns, I belly crawl along the ground until I'm an eye shot from the gunner who has his sight on the trailer while hiding behind a partially submerged barrel.

Knowing the terrain just as well as the inside of the trailer, I move silently across until I reach the edge of the water. I've checked this side of the bank and found a few gators, but it is infested with cottonmouths. They are nocturnal, though, so I don't have to worry about being bitten unless we disturb one.

I unsheathe my knife from my back holster and slowly slide into the water. One hand on the edge of the mossy bank, I move smoothly until I see who's behind that barrel.

Stupid ass. It's none other than Jig Masters, one of my competitors. The old Army Ranger has been in the business far longer than I can say. But like everyone in this business to kill, we make no friends—only money.

We've never once crossed paths, but now it's time for me to put him out to pasture.

I have no doubt Jig saw me walking in the house. But why didn't this trained killer take aim for my head right then—barely two minutes ago when he made the trailer into Swiss cheese?

However, the important question is, should I let him have an option to live or die after I question this son of a bitch?

Where common courtesy goes, there isn't. It's a do or die in this business. We follow our own rules. And first come, gets the prize. Even though I haven't pulled the trigger, Delaina Wells is mine. And no second—or third-choice hire is going to take what's mine.

Along the bank where Jig's boots dig into wet, mucky ground, a coiled cottonmouth lies. Jig disturbed it, and its body is alert in warning. I slide my arm back a few inches and take aim with my knife. I'm not going to kill it. My focus is on the killer's calf. All I want to do is cause a stir. Jig will move, the snake will bite, and I'll let the poison do my job nice and slow.

I aim, throw, and the knife lands deep in the target. The blade's dead center in Jig's calf. He grunts with pain and shifts, but it's enough that the snake strikes. Jig jerks, and the serpent strikes again at the same injured leg before slithering off in the water.

I give it a wide berth, turn, and come face-to-face with the barrel of Jig's Striker.

"You motherfucker. You think you're so smart,

Gentry." He cringes in pain, but his trigger finger remains steady.

"I always thought so," I say with a smirk.

Splashes behind me send a rivulet of worry down my spine, but I hide my trepidation.

I move closer, but Jig shakes his head. "Don't move, dickhead. I know how this will play out."

I glance down at the bite, then back to his face. "I see things differently."

He huffs out a chuckle. "I've been in the game way too long for you to fuck with me, Merrick. I'm the one who's walking away with the prize."

"That's not how it's going down, Jig. Besides, you have about five—maybe ten minutes before that venom does permanent damage and affects your nervous system, and you'll bleed out from my knife. Do you really want to sit here and debate with me? Or do you just want to kill me—like you tried to not five minutes ago." I never take my attention off this bastard.

He might be right about how long he's played the game, but I'm the one who'll walk away alive.

Sweat gleams across Jig's brow and his skin begins to look clammy. He coughs and winces, but still points his gun at me. He then yanks out my knife, blood seeping out of the wound. *Bad move.*

"You didn't happen to meet up with one of us yesterday?" Jig asks with another cough, while he struggles to sit up more.

"Why?" I ask in turn. Not giving anything away.

"You did. I know it. Boy, you are a dead man walking

now." He coughs out a laugh. His hand goes from steady to slightly shaking.

I take another step. "What's the difference? The guy encroached on my mark, so I took him out. That's the way of this business."

"No manners. You're fucked, son. That guy belonged to Mable's brood. He was her baby. Jordan was only doing recon work for her. And now, you're on her shit list. Be prepared..." Jig doesn't have to finish as he sticks out two bloody fingers from his hand that's still holding my knife, and puts them to his temple like a gun.

Fucking A. Mable Simone is the last person I want to fuck with right now. Or any of her moronic sons. She's old school. Eye for an eye and all that.

I narrow my eyes at the dying man. "Are you done, Grandpa?"

"Don't worry about me." He swallows hard. "I'll call your handler, tell him your work here is over." He gasps out a breath before he pulls the trigger.

I lunge for the gun at the same time the bullet grazes my upper arm. With a single twist, I yank my knife out of the man's hand, and knock the gun out of the other but not before Jig slams his fist to my face. I capture his injured leg and jam my thumb deep into the wound. He screams in agony and tries to wiggle out of my hold. With a firm yank, I pull Jig into the water for all of a minute, submerging him under until no bubbles escape his mouth.

Jesus. Not only do I have another two killers to look out for, but now I'll have one of the most notorious female killers after me. What the fuck am I going to do now?

4

D elaina

HOT TEARS COAT my cheeks as absolute panic sets in. Even in the small confines of the closet, the dark doesn't give me any reprieve from the scary mess I'm in. And what's with Mike with that gun?

Oh, my God. Are those more bullets?

Someone was shooting at the trailer—at me. Or whoever's shooting is after Mike. Yeah, that has to be it. I don't have friends, or enemies.

I jump as scratching from the other side of the door echoes through the tiny space.

"Stop, Treg."

More scratching.

I reach out, push the door open, and pull the dog inside with me. He whines, but I shoosh him.

I have to think. As much as I need to live in this run-down trailer, there's no way I'm going to remain here now. Not when the trailer is riddled with bullet holes.

This isn't how I see my life ending. Crouching in the back of the small closet, in the dark.

A chill rushes through me. My body can't stop shivering as I scramble for a sensible solution to this crazy situation. But trying to think of a way to get the hell out without catching Mike's attention, or the shooter's, might be impossible.

Mike told me to hide if I wanted to stay alive. I don't know if I should believe him. But the way he handled that gun, I wasn't going to argue with him.

After a long silent moment, I lean forward and press my ear to the closet door. There's nothing but quiet. Though I don't trust what I don't see or hear. I wait another five minutes before I'm positive there's no more gunfire.

Treg's whine breaks through my unsteady thoughts. He presses tighter to me, giving me several licks across my face. "Thank you, boy." Mike did one thing right. Having Treg here helps ground me.

"If Mike's dead, you're mine. And I won't be calling you Treg." He gives me another lick of approval.

There's a loud crunch and I freeze in place.

Shit. Shit—shit. That's glass.

Tightening my hold around the dog's neck, I press my body and Treg back into the farthest corner of the closet and close my eyes.

Every muscle in my body goes rigid with fear. Could it

be Mike? If it is, why sneak in the house? Why not say my name and announce that it's safe to come out?

Oh, God. Mike's dead. I know it. This is not happening.

This has to be the shooter. I hope they don't look in the closet.

Creaking floors from the hallway alert me to just how close the intruder is. A familiar squeak comes from my bedroom door. I try to stay as still as possible, but Treg starts wiggling out of my hold. "No. It's not—"

The closet door is wrenched open and a scream rips from my throat.

"I'm back." It's Mike's voice, but all I can see is from knees down—his socks and shoes are wet.

"You asshole." I slap hard at his legs.

When I look up at him, his frown is angrier than a riled hornet. I don't care if he's pissed. He has no right to scare the shit out of me like that.

"You scared the crap out of me." I crawl out of the closet and stand before I skewer the man with a glare. He's sopping wet, there's blood on his right sleeve and he has a bloody nose. "Are you okay?"

"Why did you hit me?" He growls in my face.

Totally forgetting that he's injured, my face inches closer. "Why are you angry? It's my house that has been shot up," I shout.

"No gratitude?" He backs off. "Not even a thank you for saving your life."

"Thank you? Really?" I hitch a hip and fold my arms. "Why do I need to thank you for putting my life in danger? They were shooting at you."

"Where did you get the idea that he was shooting at me?" His question is laced with annoyance.

"Because I keep to myself, and I have no friends here." I quickly realize what I just admitted about myself. Can I be any more of a loser? "I can't do this. I've had enough shit in my life, I don't need to be shot at, too. This is all your fault, Mike. You and your dog need to leave. It's not enough that I lost my job because of my asshole stepbrother, who finds every chance he can to make my life a living hell, but now the only home I have is bullet riddled."

"Your stepbrother is the one who hit you? Those bruises are from him?"

I stare at him, while the word *yes* clogs my throat. If I verbalize what happened, I might just break down, and I can't do it—can't confirm it out loud—not without shutting down completely.

Right before I turn away, Mike kisses me. Flat out grabs me by the back of the neck and slams his mouth down on mine. I'm momentarily too stunned to react. Too shocked to enjoy the heat coming off his wet body as he presses against me. Or savor Mike's taste and how his tongue dives into my mouth with absolute mastery.

The time feels infinite with his lips on me, but my brain cells finally kick in and I pull back and try to slap his face. However, he stops me before my palm meets his cheek.

"Don't ever kiss me again without my permission," I yell in his face.

His jaw tenses. "Fine," Mike says with gritted teeth and turns away.

"Fine," I huff right back, stepping away from him.

I swear there's a good minute that passes before Mike shakes his head and looks back at me. "Why do you think that Jig was shooting at me?" He folds his arms across his broad chest and scrutinizes me like I'm a pinned bug.

"Why did you kiss me?" I rattle out without thought, while still trying to shake off his drugging kiss. Needing space to breathe and think, I turn to leave without getting an answer to my question, or responding to his. "Just forget it."

Mike grabs my arm and stops me from entering the kitchen. "No. I'm not going to forget it. You were freaking out, so I helped you to refocus. Now answer my question. Why do you think someone was after *me*?"

Is this guy for real?

"Let go of my arm," I demand, yanking out of his grip.

Mike steps back, dropping his hand. "Now answer my question."

"Did you not hear what I said earlier? I don't have any friends—*or* enemies for that matter," I explain shakily, my fisted hands at my sides. My heart's pounding so hard in my chest, and I'm slightly high from the rush of adrenalin caused by being fired upon... or that damn kiss Mike planted on me.

"You don't have to have friends or enemies," Mike says coolly, but his tone suggests that he doesn't believe what I said.

"You know what? Never mind." I throw my hands up. "I don't know why I have to explain myself to you. I don't care anymore. I'm packing up my stuff and getting the hell out of Dodge."

"That's a good idea. Pack light, because I'm not sure where we're heading, or who's going to follow," Mike explains as he peels his wet shirt off and examines his injured arm.

"What? I'm not going anywhere with you. I'm leaving alone."

He gets in my face. "No, you're not. It's not safe out there. You have a price on your head, and I'm the only one who can keep you safe."

Bully tactics won't work on me, asshole. I'm too pissed right now to see reason.

Then what Mike said hits me, knocking the breath out of my lungs. "A price on my head? What are you talking about?"

"Someone put a contract on you for one million dollars, Delaina" he explains. "Now, I don't know how long we have before another killer comes looking for you, but we have to get the hell out of here."

My breath hitches and my heart ratchets up another notch at his forewarning. If he's telling the truth, do I trust this guy enough to go with him? But he has a...

My attention drifts from the gun on the counter, to his bare chest. His tantalizing wet chest.

My mind blanks out the danger as my eyes follow a drop of water from his squared off chin that drips to his muscular chest, down to the thin smattering of golden hair between the valley of his pecs.

With my mouth suddenly dry, the desire to lean in and lap up that drop becomes overwhelming.

I'm no stranger to men's physiques, but Mike's broad shoulders, his thick ropey arms, and those washboard abs—hell, I never knew eight-packs existed.

Mike snaps his fingers in my face. "We don't have time for bullshit."

I snap out of whatever lust-filled haze I'm under, stare at the stranger in front of me and decide right then that I can't be near this man. "You aren't going anywhere with me. You can take your dog and get out," I say with absolute certainty.

He grits his teeth and steps toe-to-toe with me, swallowing up whatever space was between us. That familiar ugly fear skates across my spine as Mike frowns down at me, and I freeze like a petrified rabbit.

"Do you not understand what I just said? Someone wants you dead, Delaina Wells. They put a bounty on your head for one million dollars. I'm the only one who can keep you safe. So get your bags packed, we're leaving in less than five."

His harsh demand has me reeling back like he cold cocked me in the face. An icy tendril of panic begins to take hold and I shake my head. Tears rim my eyes, blurring my vision. "That can't be."

Damn it. This isn't the time to cry.

"It is." Mike looks away as though his action proves he's telling the truth.

"Well, I don't believe you, Mike—if that is your real name," I say, my last-ditch effort to stop this insane craziness. I wipe my tears away with the back of my hand. "This is fucking nuts."

With the shitty way my week has turned out, my life can't get any worse... Can it?

I turn away from Mike, but he grabs my hand gently, and stills me. "You're right, Delaina. This is all fucked up. And I'm going to be honest. My name isn't Mike. It's Merrick. And I'm one of three hitmen who were hired to kill you."

I stumble backward, wrenching out of his hold and hitting the wall from his confession. I stare in shock at this stranger, who I let in my house. A *killer* I let in my house.

Like there's a noose around my neck, the air to my lungs is cut off. Spots dance across my vision as I slide down the wall and fall into a black abyss.

"Delaina, wake up." There's tapping on my cheek. Then warmth surrounds my body, fighting away the cold I'm feeling. I lazily open my eyes and smile.

It was all a dream.

"I'm still sleepy." I close my lids and try to stay in that warm, happy place. It was all a dream. And now I have a hot guy over me, naked, and talking to me. But I don't know what he's saying.

"Delaina." My name is like a slap to the face.

I pop open my eyes as a burst of memory—like a flash bomb—hits the rational side of my brain. I quickly scramble away from Mike when everything in the last twenty-four hours rushes back to me.

Remembering this man is here to kill me, I try to bolt off the bed but his arms wrap around my middle like iron bands and he drops me back down on the mattress. With all the strength I have, I kick and punch at him, but he's too strong.

Mike—no—not Mike, Merrick straddles my hips. He frog-legs across my thighs, preventing me from kicking him. My wrists are bound by his big calloused hands, and he's so close that I see the storm in his blue-green eyes.

"Fucking stop. Or I'm going to put a bullet in your head like I was hired to do," he spits out.

My entire body freezes from his threat.

"Please, let me go," I whisper.

"No." He shakes his head.

"Why are you doing this to me? I did nothing wrong," I plead, but he refuses to release me.

"If you step one foot out of this house without me, you *will* be dead. I'm the only one who can keep you safe," he admits with a frown.

"Who's going to protect me from you?" I throw back, remembering what he said before I passed out.

"No... I won't harm you." He shakes his head. "Listen. Someone put a hit out on you for a million."

"What?" My throat constricts with pain. The knowledge that someone wants me dead is... unthinkable. "I thought that only happened in the movies."

He huffs out a laugh as water drips off his bangs. "Let me explain this clearly to you, but you have to hear me out... And stop wiggling, damn it." He tightens his hold around my wrists and gives me a quick shake. "I'll let you go, but you have to promise me not to go off half-cocked and do something stupid."

Do I have a choice?

I gulp down the ache in my throat, my eyes welling with even more tears as I slowly nod.

"Okay." He finally lets go of my wrists and slides off me, his hands outstretched placatingly.

My eyes never leave Merrick's face as I scramble to sit against the wooden headboard, like that's going to protect me from this killer. "I knew it was going to be a shit day." I shake my head before saying, "Tell me."

"I'm what you would call a hitman. I'm hired to get rid of people."

I narrow my eyes in frustration at Merrick. "As much as I appreciate the simpleton explanation, do you think I'm that stupid? I know what a hitman is. Granted, I've never met one or wanted to, but here we are." Apparently, he doesn't appreciate my sarcasm with the way his lips tighten into a deep frown. Strangely enough, I relax under his hard scrutiny.

"I don't think you're stupid."

"Then why are you talking to me like I'm a child?" I question, scowling at him.

Merrick puts up a finger, then steps out to the hallway, makes hand signals to Treg, who the entire time has been sitting there watching us.

"Go," he says, and the dog takes off to who knows where while my hitman comes back into the room.

I let out a soft snort. *My hitman.*

I must be going crazy—to assume this guy is going to protect me. And claiming him as mine? I'm totally off my damn rocker.

"You have no clue what's coming and I don't have time for a sit down chat about who, what, and why. But I promise you, I'll have answers to any questions I can't answer now, once my handler gets me the details. But first, we need to get the hell out of here. Neither of us are safe."

I don't know this man at all. But from the grave, serious beat to his words and the harsh, pinched expression on his face, I have to believe him.

However, there's still one more question I need to ask before I step one foot anywhere with him. "Are you going to kill me?"

Merrick stills, studies me a beat with such intensity that I hold my breath, and wait for his reply.

He finally shakes his head. "This entire fucked up situation has become much bigger than just you, Delaina. So, no. But I promise you, whoever took this hit out on you, their story will have a much different ending than what they were hoping for."

I don't understand what he means, but I'm not going to argue with the man either.

"Fine," I manage to say, getting to my feet. "A hitman with morals."

"You're lucky you got me. Just imagine, if one of the other killers had you in his sights, you'd be dead. Now, pack light. You have five minutes."

His formidable demands obliterate any thread of sanity

I'm grasping on to. And as much as it pains me to admit, Merrick could be right. I'm safer with him than going at this alone.

I just pray that I'm making the right choice, because my life is in this hitman's hands.

5

M errick

As Delaina swiftly gathers her things into a backpack, I stand just inside the front door to keep watch of the driveway and the dock for any newcomers by car or boat.

Crowded by mangroves, I can't see past the cut-off of the road that leads to the trailer. And if I could hide amongst those trees along the water's edge, so can others.

Damn it. Out of all the big hitters, Mable fucking Simone and her bonehead brood are involved. Through the grapevine, I've heard her sons are relentless. And she's all about getting to the goal. The cash. With one million on the line, there's no doubt she'll be sending out her sons to kill Delaina to collect the prize.

Feeling tension down the back of my neck, I stretch it from side to side and try to remain focused. But it's difficult when my mind is swirling with ideas on how to go after Mable and her band of wayward sons. Even though I eliminated her youngest, there's still three more to look out for—not including whoever else joins the hunt to kill Delaina and, by default now, me.

I glance over my shoulder when Delaina walks out from the bedroom.

"I'm ready," she quietly says, slinging a large bag over her shoulder.

I look at what she's wearing, from her short sleeve shirt down to her open-toed sandaled feet. I shake my head. "Change into pants. Put on a long sleeve shirt and a good pair of walking shoes. We're walking through the woods and part of the Everglades."

"Why? We can jump into your car or leave in the skiff and—"

"No. Your boat isn't fast enough and we'll be easy targets out in the open. The plan is heading out back through the swamp. So don't waste what little time we have, and change," I order. Coddling isn't my deal and the sooner she knows it, the better.

"What about your truck?" She huffs out.

"It's stolen."

Her mouth drops open, closes, and opens again, but nothing comes out.

"Move, Delaina." I nudge her forward.

"Fine." She spins around and rushes out of the room with Treg by her heels.

"That must be your favorite word." The jab hits the mark because loud cursing and the slam of her bedroom door sends a spike of aggravation through my good intentions to keep her safe.

Fucking Christ. Doesn't she realize what I'm doing for her?

Then movement from the tiny dock catches my peripheral. A boat. *Shit.* I hurry to Delaina's bedroom, open the door, and find it... empty? "Damn it." After a quick glance around, I groan. "She took the damn dog."

She went out the fucking window.

I don't have time for her bullshit.

I slide one leg out of the window when an idea hits me. I need to see their faces, especially when they come after us at a different location. That way it'll be easier for me to take them out.

Tucking myself back inside, I go to the partially open front door. With a quick peek toward the water, I spot a guy dressed in camo wear, with a Sig Sauer in hand. Next to him, equal in height, mass, and similar features, is a hitter dressed the same way. They have the same facial appearance as the gator bait I killed yesterday.

These two dumb shits must be part of Mable's brood. With their faces planted in my head, I rush back to Delaina's room. After locking the bedroom door, I cautiously peer out of the window to see if it's clear. Not detecting any movements, I climb out and quickly land in a squat. Ears to the wind, there are sounds coming from inside the house.

Now, I have two choices. Either I flee and track down Delaina and my dog, or head back and take out who's inside the house.

Hearing a soft yip from my left, I swivel and see Delaina and Treg partially hidden in the dense sea myrtles. Without the white fluff, they can be easily seen through the thick branches. She's waving at me to come, but I'm still contemplating what I need to do.

Voices are now coming from inside the bedroom. I wave Delaina to hide before tucking myself back against the overgrown yew hedges.

A capped head pops out of the window. "What the fuck are you doing, asshole? Get back in here." The demand comes from inside the room.

"You don't know if they left this way, Jude," the asshole says in a hiss. He ducks his head back inside, and that's my cue to dart to where Delaina ran off to.

And not a second too soon. The other fuckwad—who I assume is Jude—rushes around the back side of the trailer, followed by the capped guy. They examine the ground under the window, but they won't find any of my footprints. I made sure of that.

"They escaped," the asshole growls.

"Mom's going to be pissed." Jude spits at the ground.

"I'm hungry," the asshole gripes.

"When aren't you hungry, Devon?" Jude scolds, before turning and heading back to the front of the trailer.

I take off over the soppy ground until I lose the sounds of the men's bitching. I follow the trail down the southern part of the property, where Delaina's muddy indents are unmistakable. Thank fuck, the two guys are idiots and won't check past the bushes, because anyone could easily spot Delaina's tracks.

I debate for a moment if I should eliminate those fuckers now or wait to get Delaina in a safe place. The best plan is to lay low, but knowing Mable, the foul-mouthed woman will be relentless in tracking us down until the mark and I are each six feet under.

If Jig was correct, with Mable calling in all her markers, she wants my head on a platter for killing one of her boys. Not only will she send in the rest of her sour brood, there are other hungry motherfuckers who will be after me.

I promise, one by one, they will be on the chopping block—if they step one foot my way. Even though this business is kill or be killed, Mable doesn't see it that way. It's all personal to her now.

With that knowing thought, I speed up my pace.

Frustration pools in my veins at the jacked-up situation I landed my ass in. If I'd only pulled the trigger, none of this shit would be in my wake. But I didn't. Now I need to keep my head on my shoulders, and at the same time make sure Delaina remains alive and find out who wants her dead.

Where to hide Delaina? I don't know. If it was only me, I'd head back home, since no one knows—not even my handler knows, where I am when I go off grid. But with Delaina with me, she would slow me down.

You can still shoot her and collect the mil.

I tell my brain to shut the hell up, and I push on.

Several yards past the dense bald cypress trees and the multiple knees jutting out from swamp water, I see a tiny rowboat at the end of a dilapidated floating dock. Inside it sits Delaina and Treg.

"This is your escape plan?" I say incredulously, examining the single ass-cheek spot reserved for me. "And I'm rowing."

Delaina frowns. "You said we can't take the other skiff. This is quiet and no one knows this is out here—even you didn't." Her dark eyes spark with haughtiness.

I growl in response. Since we don't have time to argue, I climb in and begin rowing. "Do you know how to get out of here?" Contention drips from my words.

"Yes. We have to go in that way, which will take us to highway 41." She points toward the northwest direction, and reluctantly I turn the boat that way, not having any other choice but to trust her at her word.

A good five minutes passes before Delaina breaks the silence.

"So, were those guys in my house killers, too?" Delaina asks as she glances over her shoulder to where we came from.

I contemplate how much to divulge to her. It's bad enough we're in the dark on who wants her dead. But to explain the layers of shit to her situation and about Mable's crew after us—me, in particular, I don't know if she can handle the full truth. "Yes." I then clam up, thinking my answer is enough that she won't ask any more questions.

With a pinched expression, she says, "They were the ones who shot up the trailer?"

Shit. I slowly shake my head no.

"You said you'd explain," she insists. "We have time. So, tell me."

I release a breath, knowing she's going to react badly to the truth. "Yesterday, I found a guy watching you. So, I took him out."

Her eyes go wide. "Yesterday? And what do you mean you took him out?"

I quit rowing, tucking the oars close to the boat. I lean toward her and grit out quietly, "You *know* what I mean, Delaina."

She flinches and quickly looks away. "Oh. That."

In for a pound, Aunt Winnie used to say. "Yeah, that. And the two in the trailer are brothers of the guy I killed yesterday, and they want revenge."

"Then who shot up the trailer?" she asks in a rush, unshed tears in her eyes.

I don't hesitate. "That was another guy, but I took care of him while you hid in the closet."

"How?"

The last thing I want to do is explain in detail how I killed Jig. "You don't need to know."

"So there's more than three killers out for me?" Utter panic and fear flash at me from the dark depths of her watery eyes. She's finally getting it.

"Possibly more."

"What?" Her voice hitches as tears trickle down her cheeks.

"A million dollars will attract a lot of attention. And a mark like you, it's easy money," I admit with honesty.

"I'm a mark," she mumbles, as she drops her eyes to Treg, who's hugging close to her.

Though my harsh remark causes Delaina to fold in on herself, seeing her in distress sends a fractured ache to my sternum. But it's the only way to keep her alive and focused.

A flash of realization crosses her face. Her spine stiffens as her eyes slice to me with wide shock. *Yes. She finally understands the peril she's in.*

"Oh-my-God—I have killers hunting me down—and you're one of them—and they're after you now, too, as revenge for killing their brother." She extends out an arm and pinches her leg. "I need to wake up from this night-mare." Her voice rises an octave. "Please. This can't be real. I have to wake up." She starts slapping her face. "Why?"

I grab her hands and lock them between mine. Delaina tucks her chin down to her chest and her muffled cry echoes around us.

"Quiet," I whisper, gently grabbing onto her wrist and pulling her to me, our faces inches apart. "The last thing we need is for those men to find us."

"Why, Merrick? I try to be good."

Hating to see her like this, I close the gap between us and kiss her. It's the only way to stop her from crying and making all that noise. The kiss was supposed to be short. However, the desire to taste her becomes overwhelming. When I swipe my tongue across her lips, her mouth opens in invitation.

One swipe inside her mouth, and a heady need to take

her right in the small skiff zaps me right down to my cock. I quickly pull back and stare at Delaina. She looks as lust drunk as I feel. And this is only a kiss. I can't imagine what else would develop between us if I spent enough time with this woman.

Time? Damn it. I need to stop thinking with my dick.

Getting involved with Delaina will get me killed, especially if I need to watch my back for Mable's retaliation. I have to find out who's behind the hire, snuff them out and then send her on her way.

"Why did you kiss me again?" she asks dazedly, her hand covering her mouth.

"It's the only way to shut you up." That's harsh, but the hurt on her face gives me some clarity and distance.

Delaina yanks her arm away and sits tall in her seat. She swipes at the giant tears that have slipped past her lower lashes. "I don't understand why this is happening to me. I'm a nobody."

"That's why I didn't pull the trigger, Delaina." Don't ask me why I blurt out my reservation about killing her.

The way Delaina wraps her arms around herself and shivers, I want to cocoon her and take her away from here. We can hide up in the mountains where no one will be able to find her.

Well, that sounds creepier than shit. I won't be saying that out loud.

Soft sniffles drown out the murmuring sounds of the Everglades.

If the truth will keep her safe, Delaina needs to know every detail, rather if I like her to know or not.

I grit my teeth and continue. "I've watched you for a week. You're not the normal mark that usually lands in my lap. So I reached out to my handler—"

"Your handler?" She swipes the last bit of tears with the back of her hand.

"Yeah. Joe had nothing more than what I already knew about you. So... tell me, what's so special about *you* that someone would take a million dollar hit out for your death?" I renew the rowing, but my eyes bounce from her face to where we're heading.

For the first time, without my scope, I examine her up close. Sun-kissed bronzed skin, from a mix of the Florida sunshine and her mother's Caribbean heritage. Her dark brown eyes have a slight slant at the outer corners, which comes from her father's quarter Japanese lineage.

My eyes drift from those few rich brown, loose curls framing her heart-shaped face, down to the full bottom lip she's currently biting.

I was wrong in the beginning. She isn't ordinary at all. Far from it. Delaina Wells is beautiful—and so much more.

My chest tightens at the vulnerability and exhaustion across her face, made even worse by those bruises. I blow out a breath, look away, and focus on where we're going. It's going to be up to me to keep both of us alive until I can fix what started as a simple hit. However, the biggest threat now is from me.

I need to keep my attraction to Delaina Wells tight to the vest, because one moment of distraction and I am a dead man for sure.

6

D elaina

I'm taken aback by Merrick's question. What's so special about me? That's the million dollar question—literally, that we both need answered.

But that kiss? Even though it was short, there's still a buzz of electricity running through my body. For a brief moment, when his lips were on mine, I wanted more. More of his tongue. More of his body.

However, sex won't be an option where Merrick is concerned. Not now—not ever. He came here to kill me. Granted, he promised me he won't, but can I trust his word? No. I can't trust anyone.

"What are you thinking about?" Merrick asks. His rowing speeds up.

"I don't know what's special about me, Merrick," I

answer with my chin tucked to my chest. "I've been told that I'm just ordinary and that I would get nowhere in life." I suck in a lungful of the sweltering afternoon heat, trying to calm my spiraling emotions and my racing heart. Even under the canopy of the trees, the spattering of shade doesn't lend any relief from the heat.

"Who told you that?" His light eyes go cold. "Your parents?"

"No," I rush to say, shaking my head. "My father died when I was baby. I don't remember him at all. And Mom was my cheerleader until she died when I was thirteen."

"Who took care of you after your mother died?" he asks, but I have the feeling he already knows.

"My stepdad, Brent Miller—if you can call him that. He's not been much of a father to me. He only tolerated me because of my mother."

"What about your grandparents? Weren't they there when your mother died?"

"On occasion, when I was allowed to see them."

"Tell me about your stepbrother," Merrick says with a frown.

Just thinking of Mark puts ice in my veins. "When he moved in a year after Brent and my mom got married, my life became utter hell. Mark made it clear that he hated me from the beginning and did everything in his power to hurt me."

"So, it's Brent and Mark who put all that crap in your head. Mark's the one who hit you yesterday?" The sternness of Merrick's jaw and the hard set of his ice blue eyes adds another notch to my turbulent emotions.

I nod slowly as a knot of dread churns in my belly, leaving me nauseous. "Let's drop it. I don't want to talk about Brent or my stepbrother any longer."

"Sure enough. Then tell me, who do you think wants you dead?"

My body stiffens at his question. "I don't know. I wasn't lying when I said I don't have friends. There's no family. Hardly any money in my account, and certainly no social life that would be a reason for someone wanting me to die," I say nervously, thinking of Brent or Mark putting a hit out on me. "Since you know all about me, who do you think it could be?"

"I put my nose on your stepfather, since he has the money," he assesses, and stops rowing. Merrick looks around and immediately shoots a hand out to me to keep quiet. "I hear something."

I look around us, seeing familiar markers my granddad had put on the trees when I was a child and immediately know where we are. "We're near Route 29. Another twenty minutes that way, and we can reach the dock at Copeland. Then we can find a ride on 41, and hopefully someone can give us a lift to Naples."

"Copeland? Is it a town?"

"It used be, then it turned into an outpost many years ago until the swamp ate it up. All that's left is a dilapidated building for the local Glades-men and Seminole Indians in the area," I explain as I watch the muscles in Merrick's neck work as he takes a swallow of water, and then passes the bottle to me.

"Then we head in that direction," he says and directs the boat westward.

I watch Merrick run the oar blades smoothly through the water with clean precision. Between the push and pull, I'm fascinated by the flex of his powerful shoulders, arms, and hands. I wonder if he can kill a person bare handed.

I shudder at the thought.

"Why are you looking at me like that?" With a slight tilt of his head, Merrick studies me like I'm a pinned bug under a microscope.

Should I be honest? "I'm wondering if you can kill a man with your bare hands."

The slight up tip of his lips conveys his sudden amusement. "I've come close."

I immediately straighten in my seat. "You have?"

"Yes."

"How did you come to be in this... kind of a... business?" I can't help asking. "You can do so many other things with your life."

"It's what I'm good at." He then snaps his mouth shut and that ends all conversation for the rest of the way.

It's close to thirty minutes before the boat meets the narrow dock and we all clamber off. I stretch my body from the strain of sitting so long. So does Treg before he scurries around for a place to pee.

With my bladder in near revolt, I say, "I have to go before I wet..." As I turn to Merrick, I instantly lose my train of thought when he's face-front, parked up against a tree and doing what I need to do.

The tops of his firm butt cheeks are exposed. My

mouth instantly waters and I swallow down the stabbing urge to walk up to him and pinch his ass. Instead, I turn my back and march around the rusted-out building that once used to be a small general store. Now it's nothing but a dilapidated shack for birds and other critters to hide in.

I quickly look around for a good spot before dropping my pants, squatting down and releasing my bladder.

Thanks to quick thinking on my part, I packed tissue packets and travel wipes with me. Once done, I head back to the front of the building. But not before I spot a familiar swamp flat rig approaching. It's old man Harley's boat. However, neither of the men on board is Harley.

I hurry to Merrick, who already has eyes on the twelve-footer slowly moving to the dock.

"That's Harley's boat, but those men aren't him," I quickly explain.

"I thought we'd have more time," Merrick grates, before turning to me. He gives me a light push toward the building. "Get inside and stay quiet."

"Maybe Harley knows them." I try to be positive, but Merrick shakes his head.

"No, they're the same guys who were at your house. Now listen to me and go hide." The sharp edge of his tone has me moving. Merrick gestures to Treg to go with me, and I'm grateful. Again.

I hurry inside the building and come to a quick halt, vomit threatening to spew up from the rancid smell permeating the interior. I hit the flashlight app on my cell phone and light up the dark space. Not wanting to draw attention, I aim the light down to the nasty floor.

There's rickety, cobwebbed shelving on three walls. I'm afraid if I touch any of it, it'll probably topple down on contact. The only window looking out toward the water is covered by curtains that are full of holes. At the far corner is an abandoned freezer, the lid sitting wide open.

My nose is telling me that's where the foul odor is coming from. Every step closer, the smell gets worse. Treg whines, but I hush him. As bad as the scent is, my curiosity wins out. With my hand over my mouth and nose, I aim the light inside it and regretfully see the origin. I hastily scramble back and knock into one of the shelves. The damn thing crashes to the floor, making so much noise.

Merrick told me to hide and stay quiet, but I'm not doing a very good job.

Treg starts growling, I swiftly turn off my light, and rush behind a counter. As I drop, dragging Treg with me by his collar, every nerve in my body goes taut. "Shh, boy. We need to be quiet."

Not a second later, a hulk of a man is standing in the open doorway. By the bulky silhouette of this person, I can easily see he isn't Merrick.

He stalks inside a few steps, takes out his phone and flashes the light app in my direction. I hitch a breath, hoping he doesn't see me or Treg hiding behind the glass counter.

"Come out, Delaina. I won't hurt you." The saccharin sweetness of the goon's words doesn't hide the truth of what he's going to do. He's here to hurt or kill me.

I squeeze my eyes shut, my hand grips the cell phone like it's a lifeline, and I remain quiet. But none too soon,

Treg starts growling ferociously. With valiant efforts, I try to keep the dog from bolting after the guy. The last thing I want is Treg hurt... or worse. Then Merrick would be pissed that I killed his dog.

"I promise, I'm here to protect you, Delaina. Merrick only wants you dead." The icy shift of the goon's voice doesn't match his promise or his hesitant steps toward the counter.

He's afraid of Treg.

Nonetheless, I'm trapped. What if this guy is telling the truth and Merrick is the one who's lying?

I suck in a deep breath and, on unsteady feet, I stand. He's close enough for me to see the gun in his hand, and it's pointing at my chest. My heart pounds an erratic rhythm and every bit of air in my lungs is now gone. My fingers lose their grip on Treg's collar and the dog charges.

Don't ask me why, but I hit the flashlight app on my cell and aim light in the goon's face, temporarily blinding him. The gun goes off, and I swear the bullet zings past my head.

I scream as loud as I can, and another figure emerges in the doorway. It's Merrick—I know it.

Treg clamps his jaw onto the goon's arm. He screams and drops the gun. The asshole starts punching the dog, but Merrick lets out a shrill whistle as he gets behind the jerk. Treg unclamps his teeth and backs off. Then my hitman does something I can't fully decipher in the shadowy darkness of the place.

I see a glint of silver in the goon's hands and shout, "Knife!"

Merrick collides with the goon, then wraps something around his neck. They twist about, struggling against each other before a choking sound comes from the goon's mouth. He then collapses to the ground with a gurgle.

The goon's dead and Merrick killed him. Seeing it first-hand is believing.

Merrick killed the goon with his bare hands, to protect me.

Merrick might be a killer—he proved it not one minute ago. Even with his injury from that other hitman, Merrick's a formidable protector. Without him, I won't be able to stay alive long enough to track down who wants me dead.

7

M errick

"I TOLD you to stay quiet. What words didn't you understand?" I step closer to gauge her emotions. "Delaina, did you hear me?"

She doesn't say a word, just stands there, staring at me. Then without warning, she plows into me, wraps her arms around my waist and shoves her face to my chest and starts crying. Hard.

I'm standing there in the dark, holding Delaina awkwardly in my arms. Her entire body is shaking, and I don't know what to do or say to stop her. I'm not equipped to handle anyone crying or distraught. I go, shoot, and get out. That's it. Kissing her isn't in the cards either. Her taste is too much of a distraction. I need to keep my wits about me.

"I'm sorry, Merrick," she hiccups and separates herself from me. "Where's the other goon?"

"Goon?" I restrain myself from laughing.

"Yes. That other guy."

"He's dead," I say point blank, all humor gone. I'm not going to explain how I got rid of the other brother by hiding in the river oats grasses. Then I jumped out, surprising the dick, and sliced his neck before drowning him in the water. Yeah, Delaina doesn't need to know that.

They have similar features. No doubt, these two fuckers are Mable's boys. Now I have killed three... for Delaina Wells.

"Okay." Delaina stares at my shirt. She then doubles over and throws up.

I reach for her, but a bite of pain radiating from my left shoulder stalls me.

Delaina extends a hand and stumbles back. "I'm good."

I track where her eyes are glued, glance down and see blood soaking my shirt. The bone-edged knife that fucker tried to fillet me with sliced through my skin, though the damage is minimal. Most of the blood on me is from the guy I used my garrote on.

Delaina straightens, as her eyes rove over my body. "You're bleeding, a lot," she says more steadily. "I brought my first aid kit." She retrieves her bag and pulls out a small green case.

"It's not all my blood." I eye the box.

Delaina pulls out a package of wipes, a tube of ointment and gauze pads before stepping toward me. "Let me see."

I distance myself. "I'm fine. And we don't have time to dally."

"Dally?" Her eyebrows hike up to her hairline. She steps to me, rips the sleeve, and starts wiping at my wound. "If you're going to keep me safe and alive, then I need to keep you safe and healthy," she snorts. "Dally."

"It's what my Aunt Winnie used to say to me," I rush out, not realizing what I just openly admit. I clamp my teeth tight as the burn from the cleaning shoots down my arm.

"Your Aunt Winnie? Is she the one who told you about the funny bone?" she asks with a cheeky smirk, all the tears from minutes before are wiped dry. But her smile quickly fades when she looks up at me. "Merrick, I won't tell anyone about you—I promise."

"I know you won't." I remain still as she continues to wipe away the blood.

"Sounds like you were fond of your aunt." She blows out a breath. "Now take off your shirt. It's easier for me to wrap a bandage around your arm."

I let out a grunt. "We don't have time for this." But I do her bidding and pull my shirt over my head. I stare at her wide-eyed expression before twisting my head toward the dock and briskly scanning the perimeter. I don't see anything or anyone. I turn back around and ask, "Done yet?"

"Um... Nope," she says breathily but immediately clamps her mouth shut. Her eyes graze down my body with apparent heat. She blows out a breath and refocuses on my arm. Delaina is a smart cookie. There's more to this woman than just good looks and a rocking body—Wait. Her body is the last thing I should be thinking about or looking at.

"Hurry up. We need to get out of here," I press, meeting her dark eyes. "Why didn't you go to nursing school?"

Delaina's silent while she works quickly on the small bandage.

But I already know the answer behind it. Unexpectedly, I feel the need to track down her stepfather and stepbrother and pull the fucking trigger. I'd do it for free.

"I know what you're thinking."

"No, you don't," I say evenly.

"Then what?" She studies my face. Between the touch of her gentle fingers on my skin and the taste of her lips still branded on mine, my dick suddenly demands attention. I pull out of her hold the second she steps back and turn around so as not to expose what's tenting my pants.

"We don't have time to stand here and chit chat." I stalk to the bags where Mable's boys stashed their shit. Finding some jerky, a couple of water bottles, and a couple of clean shirts, I slip a white t-shirt on and transfer the rest to one bag. "Get your bag while I clean up..." I don't finish.

"Clean up what—" She looks around before her eyes shoot to me. "Don't tell me. I don't want to know."

I don't. Delaina hastily packs up while I dispose of the second body, and we're soon ready to take the flat boat out.

"All right?" I ask, while scanning the waterway.

"Yes," Delaina says before climbing in, with Treg right behind her. She takes a seat, and my dog sits next to her.

Delaina's slightly pale and definitely exhausted. I don't know how long she can maintain this pace. I have to figure out how to get her out of Florida.

Once we get onto Harley's boat, she releases a small smile that doesn't ease the tension in my chest. Even with the reassurance and honest trust on her face, something in me cracks.

Damn it, Merrick. Keep your eye on the goal, not on the girl.

8

M errick

Riding through the Glades, I try calling Joe on my cell, but it won't go through. I would have used Delaina's phone, but she accidently dropped it in the water a mile back.

No matter. I doubt there's any cell reception out here anyway.

We come to an impasse and have to lose the boat five miles from our destination and hike the rest of the way. It's nearly one in the afternoon when we finally reach the outskirts of Copeland.

By the time we reach the gas station on Route 41, Delaina's heel has a giant blister. She's in the bathroom cleaning up, while I'm outside trying to reach Joe again. I dial, and the call finally goes through.

"Where the fuck have you been? I've been trying to call you," Joe impatiently huffs through the phone.

"*You* hung up on me, asshole," I snarl into the cell. My fingers curl tight around the phone, and the urge to strangle my handler doubles.

"Sorry. You don't normally ask about the marks—" he pauses, letting out a loud sigh. "Yet that doesn't mean your lack of following through on this job isn't merited. Now, catch me up. Where are you? Did you kill her yet?"

Sometimes, I really want to track this bastard down and kick his ass. But other times Joe sounds so reasonable, I think twice about putting a bullet in his skull.

"We got caught up with more of Mable's boys," I explain, while I keep watch on the single road and Treg, who's whining for Delaina.

"What do you mean *we*?"

"Me and—"

"No fucking way." His whiny growl of displeasure puts my teeth on edge.

"Let me explain—"

"You have a mil on the line and you're throwing it away over a woman. What happened? Did she suck your dick so good that you changed your mind about wasting her?"

Joe's verbal talons dig deep, and my fingers tighten even more around the cell, pretending it's his neck. "You wait one Goddamn second. You have no fucking clue what's going on and now you throw that shit out on me? Remember, Joe, I fucking pay your bills. One hit won't hurt your pocketbook."

"It's a mil, Merrick. It's not chump change."

"I don't fucking care."

"You should," he shrills back.

"Why?" I growl.

"Because Mable is out for you," Joe says as though I should be shocked by the news. I'm not. She's already set two of her boys on me.

"That bitch is calling in all her markers."

"I don't give a fuck. I won't put a bullet in anyone's head who is innocent. Got me?"

"You know for a fact your mark is unstained?" Doubt mixed with anger radiates through his question.

"I do," I say with confidence. Even if I don't know Delaina at all. Being in her presence for a short time, that woman doesn't have an evil bone in her body.

"Then as your handler, I'm telling you right now that you're fucked."

"Then I'll deal. In the meantime, I need your help."

Joe's insufferable grunts from the other end of the line raise the hair on the back of my neck. "Merrick... I..." The phone line goes dead, and I go on total alert.

"Joe," I grate out, quickly redialing the asshole's number. The call goes straight to voicemail. I'm about to throw the phone against the building but think better of it. I shove the cell into my pocket and aim to get Delaina out of here, and fast.

I glance around for anything suspicious. Nothing. I got rid of three of Mable's sons—If she's a smart woman, she'll keep her last son out of my way.

Tension radiates from my shoulders like a taut band across my back, knowing we are on our own.

Delaina comes out soon after, with an armful. I eye the bag.

"I'm hungry," she says with a shrug. "So what did your handler say?"

"He can't help," I spit out, still annoyed with the abrupt cut off from Joe's call. It doesn't matter if I don't get his help, I need to get Delaina to safety—I don't care where—before someone else takes a shot at us.

"What do you mean, he won't help? I thought he was there for you," Delaina says as she pops a triangular chip into her mouth.

"What we need to worry about is finding a ride to the next big city where I can retrieve some cash, find a car and get us out of Florida." I scan the gas station's lot and spot two trucks, a compact car, and some people getting gas. "I think I found us a ride."

"With whom?" Delaina asks as she tosses a piece of dried jerky to Treg.

"Be right back—and stop feeding him that. He'll get gas."

"Merrick." But I ignore her and focus on an old man and woman who might be talked into giving us a ride to the next town, which from my memory is Everglades City.

"Excuse me, sir." I approach with ease and calm civility.

"Yes?" The elderly man assesses me with his narrowed amber eyes and a note of unease in his hunched stance.

"I'm sorry to bother you, but my wife and I aren't from

around here. Our car broke down five miles back and we had to hike all this way to call in a tow truck. I was wondering if we can grab a ride with you in the back of your truck to the next town?" I point to Delaina, who in turn waves at us. "That's my wife and dog."

"I don't think..."

"You look like nice folks. Why not, Fred," the wife says with a gentle smile for her husband. "It's our Christian duty to help the ones in need."

"I can pay for the gas?" I suggest. When I pull out a hundred from my wallet the man perks up.

The old man stares at the money for a short moment before he agrees. "Okay." He snatches the bill from my fingers and pockets the cash. I wave to Delaina to come over.

"I'm Fred Warden and this is my beautiful wife, Linda."

"Hello, I'm Delaina Wil—"

"Delaina Willow Gent. And I'm Mike Gent," I interrupt. Delaina narrows her dark eyes at me and then quickly pastes on a too wide grin and shakes the couple's hands.

We intend to sit in the bed of the pickup. Instead, the old couple offers us the back seat in the cab. It's going to be a cramped ride with Treg in the middle, but we graciously accept and get in.

"You know the next town is Everglades City, but if you need a bigger city, we're heading to Naples to visit our grandkids," Linda graciously suggests.

"If you don't mind, Naples would be perfect," I admit with a glance at Delaina.

"Thank you so much for your help," Delaina says with a genuine smile, which lights up the golden flecks in her ebony eyes. How come I never noticed those before?

"You are so welcome, my dear." The old woman pats Delaina's hand that's resting next to the headrest. "You look like big city folks. Where are you from?"

Before I get a chance to lie, Delaina says, "We're from Chicago."

"We've been there. Too busy and way too noisy for my liking," Linda admits with a scrunched up face.

"But I do love their deep dish pizza," Fred says with a wagging finger in the air.

"They do have good pizza," I admit, but my eyes remain on Delaina. I try to convey to her, the less we say the better for all of us. But her attention is fixed ahead.

The couple chatter away, with Delaina joining in on their conversation. I remain quiet but stoic while keeping an eye out for any tag-a-longs. It helps pass the hour until we hit the center of Naples, between Routes 41 and 75.

"Thank you so much for the ride," Delaina conveys to the elderly couple.

"You're most welcome. And I hope you get your car fixed. Take care now." Linda waves goodbye and Fred drives off down Main Street.

A glimmer of happiness stirs in Delaina's eyes as she watches the couple drive away. "I hope one day I'm that happy with the one I love."

Her words hit something deep in me as I trace the vanishing smile on Delaina's face. What is it about this woman that captures my attention? In the last week—the last twenty-four hours—she's lost her job because of her fuckwad of a stepbrother, and her only home is full of bullet holes. Not to mention that several killers are out to collect a boon for her death, and now she's on the run with me.

Maybe a bullet to the brain would have been kinder than what she has to face in the next several days—or weeks. It will depend on how fast I can cut Mable's retaliation at the knees and find out who's behind Delaina's hit.

"Merrick?" My name on her lips stirs something primal in me that I have never felt before. The need to protect Delaina Wells is becoming more of a selfish reason than I want to admit. "Merrick."

"What?" I growl, refocusing back on her face.

"Wouldn't you want to be happy like that couple some day?" The vulnerability across her watery dark depths puts an ache in my chest I'm not liking.

"Today isn't the day. And why are you crying?" I hate to burst her bubble, but when killers are hunting us down, I need to keep my head clear and sharp, or we're dead standing here. "We need to get somewhere hidden so I can regroup."

Especially with Joe's call being cut off, I don't know if it's his normal ploy or if it's disloyalty. He's pissed that I didn't kill Delaina, but in my gut, I know there's more. I just don't know what.

My disposable phone pings with a text. There's only one person who has this number. I glance down and it's an unknown number. With a quick swipe of the screen, I open the app and see Joe's message.

Joe: *Dude. I was cut off. A hacker infiltrated my system and all my shit is fucked.*

Me: *How do I know this is you?*

Joe: *BA-HOP.*

I grunt out a laugh, relief settling my anger.

"Who's that?" Delaina peers down at the screen. "What does BA-HOP mean?"

"It's an acronym for Bad Ass Hacker On Patrol. It's his code to let me know it's really him when shit goes fu-bar."

"Fu-bar? Seriously?" She chuckles. "I don't know what that is but I'm guessing it's bad."

Another ping draws my attention.

Joe: *Are you still there?*

Me: *Sorry. Quickly tell me what's going on.*

My phone rings this time and I pick it up.

"Dude. Shit is messed up. My system got hacked and... that Mable bitch is out for blood. So I'm right. She wants to take you down with no prejudice."

"We're in Naples. Need cash and a car," I say, while my mind tries to scramble out a solution. I glance over to Delaina, who's biting her lower lip. Without thought I reach out, taking the pad of my thumb to stop her nervous habit.

Soft and plump to the touch. I wonder—I quickly shake that thought out of my head.

Delaina's eyes widen, and a spark of need in them hits me dead center in my groin. I promptly step back and turn my back on her before my dick stands at full salute.

"I'm telling you, Merrick. You and your woman need to hide," Joe says, as I glance over my shoulder at her.

"She's not my woman," I blurt out, catching the flinch on her face.

"Whatever, dude."

"I want you to track down who wants her dead. That is your only focus right now, Joe. I'll take care of Mable and the hitters that come our way."

"Fucking shit. Merrick..."

"Just keep digging into who put out that contract. Got it?" I convey the order with no room for excuses.

"Give me a clue?"

"Check Brent Miller's finances." My admission elicits a gasp from Delaina. Feeling slightly exposed standing out in the open, I quickly look around.

"That's it?"

"I want a full breakdown on Mark Miller."

"The stepbrother?"

"Yeah. I have a feeling there's a connection there," I say.

"It's going to take some time since I'm working on an old system," Joe growls out his displeasure.

"I have every confidence in you to find out. In the meantime, call me only when you have news."

"You got it." Joe hangs up.

I turn to Delaina, who's a couple of yards away. Immediately not liking the distance between us, I close the gap. My hands itch to touch her, but I keep them at my sides.

Delaina's attention is directed down the street. I follow

where her eyes are fixed and come to a quick conclusion. "We need to find a place to lay low until tonight."

"How about that one?" She points to the small motel a half block down from where we're standing.

"It's low key. Perfect."

Delaina doesn't say a word but follows along until we reach the motel's glass door. There's a tiny, unassuming note in the window that reads, *available pay-by-the-hour rate*. It's the epitome of what a seedy motel would post, but in a slightly upscale motel off the strip.

I inwardly scoff, knowing exactly the kind of people that take advantage of that bit of detail. With hurricane Mable bearing down on us, we may only have a few hours until more killers track us down. It's imperative Delaina rests until we get out of here.

"Wait here with Treg while I get us a room," I relay, but still there's no response from her. All she does is nod, then turn away and stare toward the busy street.

Hmm. She's mad about something, but I can't worry about it now. With cash I stole from the goons, I quickly get a room at the very end of the building. Without a word, Delaina follows closely behind until we reach room twelve.

"We have the room until eight tonight," I explain as we near the door. "By then, I'll have more cash and a vehicle."

Delaina pauses and extends a hand. "Where's my room key?"

I glare at her over my shoulder. "We're sharing a room and I'm not arguing with you about it." I open the door, step inside, and immediately get bombarded by smoke, stale beer, and mildew. Treg trots in and begins sniffing around.

"I can't stay in the same room with you," Delaina declares from the doorway.

"You have no choice. Now get in here before someone sees you standing there and decides to put a bullet through you."

My words catch fire because Delaina rushes inside the room and slams the door.

9

D elaina

MY HEART'S pounding against my ribcage as I plaster myself against the closed door and look wildly around the room. Even the foulness of the space doesn't dispel the spike of panic shooting through me.

Suddenly my vision narrows, and all the energy in my body is gone, along with the air in my lungs. With a shudder, the entire room shrinks into a tiny pinprick. Then a solid wall of chest blocks my blurry view of the room. My head tips back and I stare up at Merrick's handsome face that's inches from mine.

"Breathe, Delaina. Yes, that's it. Breathe."

I barely catch the gentleness of his voice. But for some reason I listen to him and take an unsteady breath. "You... are... an... asshole."

"I know. One more," he orders in a whisper, his lips a millimeter from mine. If I lick my lips, the tip of my tongue will surely touch his mouth.

I center my focus on Merrick's eyes and mimic his steady breathing. A rough wet tongue brushes against my fingertips. Treg plasters his body against my legs, giving me a bit of comfort.

As my vision widens, I slowly suck in a lungful of nasty air. All the while, my eyes remain on Merrick, who studies me with concern.

The tender way his fingers slowly massage my scalp sends gooseflesh across my skin. I hate how achy my sex is and I want to push him away for making me feel helpless and aroused at the same time. I swallow back a soft groan as a tingly sensation ripples down my back and the tightness in my chest slowly eases. That delicious pulse between my legs grows and I'm suddenly aware of how attracted I am to Merrick. My hitman.

Merrick gives me a slight shake. "Are you okay?"

"I'm okay," I admit, trying to pull out of his hold.

"You sure?" Merrick asks, doubt cresting his beautiful eyes. He doesn't step back or give me space, for which I'm grateful, since my legs still feel weak. Yet he's the one who's making me shiver for a whole different reason.

The longer we stand close, the more the heat from his body steadies me, which contradicts how emotionally unstable I am. My body yearns for his touch, but my mind hates Merrick for intruding in my space.

"Yes." I lick my dry lips and his eyes automatically track my tongue. For the barest moment, I think he's going to kiss me again. My pulse kicks back up but I refuse to submit to my desire. "Merrick." His name slides out of my mouth in a wanton plea.

"Delaina," he says like smooth, aged scotch. His entire body goes solid before Merrick steps away from me and rushes to the door. "I have to get cash and scope out a vehicle. Don't leave the room or open the door for anyone. Got it?" The stern determination across his brow isn't something to ignore.

"Yes," I say with averted eyes, but my stomach wants to revolt at the idea of him leaving me here alone.

"Treg." The hard command has me holding my breath.

God, he's taking the dog. A small amount of fear skates through me, but I won't let it show—not in front of this man.

As Merrick reaches the door, Treg trots over to his side. I clamp my mouth shut from protesting, as both man and animal pass the threshold and he swiftly shuts the door.

I slump against the wall, unwanted tears welling in my eyes. The worry that Merrick might not come back spears my mind like a harpoon. With each slow breath, I try to push down my anxiety.

"You're made of stronger stuff, Delaina," I whisper the words my grandma used to say to me as I wipe away the wetness with both hands.

Staring at the door, my eyes drift to the two double beds covered in cheap brown and green striped coverlets that are reminiscent of the seventies style. The once white walls are now stained yellow from tobacco smoke. The room reeks of it. Dropping my attention to the atrocious dark green carpet, I don't have to see the cesspool of germs lying dormant between the fibers to know not to walk on the rug with bare feet. If I have to, I'll sleep with my shoes on.

The second my words penetrate my brain, a peel of laughter bubbles out of me. I double over, snort and laugh again. As crazy as it looks, I can see the humor—what little of it there is—and I have to laugh the fear, tiredness, and worry out of my body. Or I'll break down from the severity of my circumstances.

"What's so funny?"

I snap my head up and stare at Merrick, who's standing in the doorway with a frown on his face. Damn. I didn't hear him open the door or come into the room.

"Nothing." I shake my head. "You're back so soon."

He quickly closes the door.

Is that guilt across his face?

"I forgot to ask if you're hungry. I'm going to pick up some food." His eyes are everywhere but on me.

I have a feeling that's not what he wanted to ask me, but I go with it. "I am, a little."

"Anything special?"

"Whatever's fine. I'm not fussy," I admit with a partial smile, which quickly disappears when he doesn't return it.

"Okay. Treg, stay here." Merrick storms out of the room with a hard close of the door.

I glance down at the dog, who looks at the door and then to me with a soft yip. "I don't get it either, boy." I rub his head for reassurance, which in turn makes the dog bark again.

Not wanting to dwell on what's up Merrick's butt, I decide to take a hot shower to scrub off the day's sweat and dried mud from hoofing through the wetlands. I gather my clean clothes and socks, and head into the bathroom.

The room may look old, but the bathroom isn't dingy—however, one can't say *hot* is what came out of the pipes. The water was barely warm enough to wash the dirt off my body and clean my hair.

Feeling a whole lot better, I dress and step out of the bathroom with a towel wrapped around my head, only to be greeted by a man in a black ski mask with a gun aimed straight at me.

10

Merrick

WHAT THE FUCK is wrong with me?

I shouldn't be feeling guilty for what's happening to Delaina. I'm not the one who put a hit out on her. However, the defeated look across her face and her watery eyes slashed at my heart harder than anything I have encountered in my life, aside from losing Aunt Winnie.

"Fuck," I grunt, my jaw locking tight from gritting my teeth. There's never been a moment where I have been guilty for my actions, until her. She's the mark that might get me dead, if I don't clear my fucking head and pay attention.

Crossing Main Street, I head to the ATM outside of the local bank a block from the motel. Relieved that I'm able to pull five hundred out of my account, I tuck the bills in the front pocket of my pants and head to the next stop. The car rental place on the map app on my phone shows it's a few blocks west of here.

I make it a half a block down when I hear barking. Every inch of my body draws up, immediately knowing that it's Treg. I bolt back toward the motel and spot my dog viciously scratching at the door and yowling.

As I draw close, making sure I don't have witnesses, I pull out the 9 mm tucked at my back and quickly screw on the silencer. Approaching the room, I call Treg to calm. He immediately stops barking and sits.

I lean against the door to listen, but I don't hear anything, which disturbs me. With a swift kick to the door, it opens with a crack. I give the signal to Treg to check, and he goes straight to the bathroom. My stomach lurches.

"Fuckity-fuck." I rush to the bathroom, but there's no Delaina. The window is busted out, and when I slide a finger across the shower wall, it comes away wet. Whoever took her hasn't been gone too long. The question is, how far did they go?

Calling Treg, I grab the shirt Delaina wore today and put the fabric to my dog's nose. "Find her, boy."

Treg takes off, with me right on his tail. We're five blocks over, in a deserted alley where the dumpsters are lined up for the businesses a street over. I spot a tall, hulking guy with a skull cap, carrying Delaina over his shoulder. She reminds me of a rag doll as the asshole jostles her with every rapid step.

I stop, take aim—making sure the bullet hits the prick

right on the knee. With a single breath in, I hold it and squeeze the trigger with confidence.

A loud grunt and a stumble from the son of a bitch has me moving forward. When he drops Delaina on the pavement, Treg latches onto the guy's arm. I take aim again, waiting on his next move. I don't know who this fucker is, but with one look at his face, I'd bet my life he's not part of Mable's brood, but a hire.

A glint of silver catches my attention, and I quickly call Treg to heel. My dog releases his jaw off the fucker's arm and starts circling around Delaina.

If the asshole's smart enough, he'll freeze on the spot. But deep in my gut, I know he's going to do something stupid.

Sure enough, with his back to me, he whips out a gun and takes aim. Not at me, but at Delaina. I don't stop to think and just pull the trigger. He goes down with a bullet to the side of the head. In those few crucial seconds, I canvas the area.

Thank fuck, I had on the silencer, or the sound would have drawn attention from onlookers the next block over. I quickly text Joe to wipe out the camera footages from the back of the stores. He responds with a thumbs up.

I then rush to Delaina, who's still out cold, but is breathing evenly. Knowing she's safe, I drag the guy behind a dumpster, making sure he won't be found until garbage day, whenever that is.

After picking through his pockets, I find cash and a burner phone, and I take both. Then I pick Delaina up, cradling her in my arms, and carry her back to the motel.

Now more than ever, we need to get the hell out of Florida. Making sure she's secure, I break into the room next to us and find it empty. I place Delaina in bed and then move the rest of her shit over.

Since I won't be gone long, and with Treg on guard, I take a chance and literally run to the car rental place. On the short race there, I come to the realization the only safe place for Delaina is in Vermont. With me. It'll be a trek, but I know I can protect her on my land.

With the key to an unobtrusive vehicle, I drive the gray minivan to the motel. If we blend in, there might be a good chance I can reach home without using any more of my bullets. But that depends on what Mable has in store for me.

I just hope that I can retrieve my rifle and bag from the truck I left by Delaina's home without any more issues. But hope is the operative word.

11

D elaina

WET LICKS on my face aren't what I'm expecting as I slowly wake from a dream filled with a naked Merrick doing dirty things to me.

"Treg, stop," I mutter, pushing the dog off my lap. But then a memory flashes to the guy in our motel room. I jolt upright in panic. Still disoriented, I gulp out a fearful cry, "The guy..."

"Whoa, you're safe, Delaina." Merrick's hand grips onto my shoulder, his voice lending a steady ease to my frantic mind.

My eyes rivet to Merrick's stern face as he hovers over me. I quickly suck in a calming breath and look around. "Merrick?"

"Relax, you're safe," he says as his eyes rove over my face. "How are you feeling?"

"Like my head's underwater." I take another slow inhale as my heart steadies from its thrashing against my ribcage. "Where are we?" I ask, realizing I'm in the back seat of a minivan. It's dark outside and I can't see where we're at.

"Just past Atlanta," Merrick says as he looks out the back window. "Here's some water. Are you hungry?" He shoves a granola bar and a bottled water into my hands.

I drop the bar in my lap, but unscrew the bottle and gulp down half the contents to wash away the sandy grit from my mouth and throat.

"Slow down or you're going to make yourself sick."

"What happened?" I finally ask, trying to put the missing pieces of my memory together. "Where's the guy..." I blink back the onset of tears and swallow down the creeping ache in my throat.

Merrick's jaw tenses before he leans in close. There's anger in his unblinking eyes. "I don't know who he was, but you were lucky he didn't shoot you dead on the spot."

My entire body shudders at Merrick's declaration. I hold back the bile that's threatening to come up. "The last thing I remember is getting out of the shower and finding him in the room. I don't know how he got Treg outside, but he came after me and... that's all I remember," I confess, still muddling through my scattered thoughts.

"He must have chloroformed you before carrying you out of the motel room. As for Treg, I still can't figure that part out. But don't worry, that'll be the last time I'm leaving you alone." The hard determination across his brow gives me some comfort. Yet, I'm still not a hundred percent sure that he won't shoot me in the near future.

I glance out the window to see a passing car. I think we're on the side of a highway. "Where are we going?"

"My place."

"Your place?" I straighten, and another wave of nausea skates across my stomach.

"Yes," Merrick replies decisively before climbing out of the back. He shuts the sliding door and then climbs into the driver's seat.

"Where's that?" I finally ask while petting Treg's head for comfort. God, I love this dog.

Merrick's eyes meet mine in the rearview mirror. "Buckle up."

A ball of frustration knocks around in my gut at his non-answer. I suck in a cleansing breath before I buckle up.

With Treg next to me, between the rear captain chairs, I slump back and keep my eyes to the window, totally ignoring Merrick.

I must have fallen asleep because I wake to the straining light of dawn peering through the vehicle windows. I slowly sit up and take in the view. There's nothing but high ranges of hills, forests of different shades of green, and a small white cottage style house nestled several yards away from where the minivan is parked.

For several seconds, I'm taken aback by the scenery. Then the realization that I'm alone in the minivan kicks up my panic. However, my fear quickly subsides as I see Merrick coming toward the back of the vehicle.

I don't get how he settles my nerves, especially since the reason why we're here together is because of a hit taken out on me. But I try not to dwell on that bit of detail too long.

"You're finally up," he says, a slight grin hitches on his handsome face. "You looked so peaceful that I didn't want to wake you." There's lightness in his blue eyes and his broad shoulders are loose like the entire world isn't weighing on him. No, that part is all on me.

"You should have woken me," I say with a sudden yawn.

"You needed sleep."

"I feel like I had *too* much sleep," I counter, feeling surly for no reason.

"Apparently not enough when I stopped twice before we got here and you didn't move for either stop." Merrick chuckles as he pulls out a large black duffle bag and a long rectangular case from the back.

"Really?" I utter, while getting out of the vehicle. Latching eyes on the black case, I wonder if there's a gun inside it. "What is that?"

"It's my gun. I had to backtrack to your place to retrieve it, along with the rest of my gear."

"I must have been *that* tired, not to wake up," I admit with shrug. "What about your vehicle you left on my property?"

"Don't worry about it." It's all Merrick says before

swinging the duffle onto his shoulder. Grabbing the long case in his other hand, he strides back to the house.

"Why do you do that?" I hate his brisk answers. Hell, I hate everything about the man and this entire situation... Okay, hate is a harsh word, but in my current mood, it fits.

Keep lying to yourself. You know you want to see what's underneath those well-worn jeans, too.

"Do what?" There's a note of humor in his voice, which adds fuel to my frustration. My sudden desire to see this man naked quickly dies a fast death.

I fold my arms across my chest and glare at him. "Forget it," I huff out.

He pauses mid-step, turns, and stares at me like I have two heads. "I don't know what the hell you're talking about. You asked a question. I answered it. I don't need to go into flowery prose for you to get it." He spins back around and stalks off toward the house.

I snort. Loudly. "Flowery prose? Hah. You sound like an old lady. Just forget it. Fine. I'll stop asking questions. Just walk away." I shout at him, purposely picking a fight. But he doesn't bite, which only pisses me off more. "Jerk."

Now I'm stuck here, in the middle of God knows where, with a hitman that might try to shoot me instead of saving me like he promised.

12

M errick

ONE WHOLE MONTH goes by and not a hint of Mable's boys sniffing around my property. Don't get me wrong, I'm elated for Delaina's sake, but I can't be lax on what I cannot see.

Still on alert, I won't let anyone get to Delaina—not if I can help it. However, I don't know how long my efforts will last. I barely sleep a few hours a night. Always on guard. Even Treg is diligent when we hike the area to make sure my land is clear.

With my animal traps set throughout my property, if those assholes decide to step one foot on my land, they're in for some nasty surprises.

Mable has been in this business way too long for me to not take her serious. She has too many connections in the black underbelly of the dark web. There's no doubt that woman won't give up until I'm six feet under for taking the life of her boy. Then she'll collect the prize once she kills Delaina.

But a month in? With no peep out of her and what's left of her ugly brood? I don't trust the quiet, or her.

Granted, I'd rather deal with Mable's sons than face Delaina. From the start of each day, every time we're in the same room, we're facing off about one thing or another.

"There's no tv." Or, *"How come it's too cold in the house?"* Or *"Why isn't the hot water working? Why can't I go for a walk?"*

Those are the daily questions I get from her. I want to pull my fucking hair out.

Every time we argue, my dog runs out of the room. I don't blame the animal, I'd do the same fucking thing, if I could.

It doesn't help when I've tried several times explaining to her about the heat and wood stove in the living room. But that isn't enough. Or that she can't go for a walk for her own safety. There are too many unknown variables I can't control once she steps out of the house.

And now, as I'm sitting outside by the front door, she's probably inside bitching about something else... Laundry, maybe.

I'm regretting not shooting her... *No, I'm not.*

Guilt trickles in for thinking that way, I blow out a steady breath and stare out at the vast view of my property. From the rolling hills to my west, the glorious shades of green from the trees that rooted to this land, and to the setting skyline of orange, red and blue. Peace eases into me like a familiar warmth of home.

Truth is, if I have to admit it out loud—which I won't, Delaina's presence in the house is refreshing. She kind of reminds me of ... "Aunt Winnie." I clamp my teeth tight and shake my head at that revelation.

My aunt always bitched about one thing or another. I remember her complaining about needing another wood stove for the upstairs, so the bedrooms would be warm. I also recollect that she had contemplated getting solar panels too, so she could get a washer and dryer inside this place, instead of lugging the clothes to town where there's a laundromat.

My shoulders slump and my head dips in regret as more memories singe at the periphery of my mind. I have no excuse for my stupidity and ignorance back then, and now.

Yet, I should have fixed those things for Aunt Winnie before she died, but my head was too full of my own wallowing shit that I hadn't seen to her needs.

Winnie gave me back my life. Taught me so much about the world, about trust, and to live the best I know how. And not once did I give back to her—not in the way I should have. All the things that needed fixing, I did, after I came back home from military.

Got those solar panels, so I could do laundry here. I haven't had a chance to put in a heater for the upstairs. But that's next on my list.

I'm sorry, Aunt Winnie. My head tips back and I stare at the darkening sky. "I'm sorry."

A crash inside the house and a yelp from Treg has me jumping to my feet and rushing into the house toward the back room where I store all of the canned and dry goods. My heart throttles up as I see broken glass jars, and the food that was once inside them, are all over the floor.

A quick glance over my shoulder and I see Treg perched by the stairs, away from the mess. But Delaina is not. Standing in the center of all that mess, her mouth agape and eyes wide, she's staring at the shelving unit tilted on an angle against the opposite wall. She then meets my eyes with a remorseful wince.

"I...I didn't... mean—I mean—I'm sorry. I wanted to make dinner for you, and I was trying to grab the jar of pasta sauce from the top shelf to make pasta, but I couldn't reach it. So, I climbed on the shelf thinking I can get it, and I guess I was... well, too heavy for the shelves and it toppled forward." She winces again, and wrings her hands thoroughly. "I'm sorry—crap, I said that already." She clamps her lips shut, her eyes filling with unshed tears.

I want to be mad, but I can't. She's torturing herself enough that she doesn't need my berating. As long as she isn't hurt, it doesn't matter about the food. That stuff can be replaced, but her...

I let out a sigh and extend a hand. "Come on, before you cut yourself." I take her hand and help her avoid the glass shards and lead her out of the back room.

"I really am..." The tears she has been holding back begins to fall.

Without considering her feelings about being touched,

I pull Delaina into my arms, tuck her under my chin and wrap her tight in my hug. "I said it's okay."

Within three beats, her face plasters to my chest, and she bursts into tears. I don't say another word, remembering what Aunt Winnie had said about women needing a good cry once in a while. So, I let Delaina do just that.

Treg is at our side in an instant, leaning against us, mainly Delaina's leg. He's whimpering for a head scratch. Not sure if he needs the connection from me or Delaina, but I reach down and rub his head. So does Delaina, which seems to ease my dog's tension.

Once Delaina calms, I pull her to the couch and sit her down. "Sit, and let me clean up the mess."

"No. I should." Delaina tugs on my hand as she tries to stand. But I still her with my other hand on her shoulder.

"No. You sit." I don't say anything else and proceed to clean up the mess while she sits in the living room, with Treg curled up next to her.

Thankfully, not all of the glass jars are broken, and all of the boxed items are intact and clean from red sauce that splashed all over the place like a splatter art painting.

"Want help?" Delaina peers around the corner, her eyes glassy. The guilt is written all over her face. In that moment, my seesawing emotions for this woman solidify into something I don't want to decipher. Not yet anyway. Not until we're both safe.

I could have just walked away from this contract. Walked away from Delaina. But I knew after one look at her beautiful face from under the mangrove roots. Not now.

Not ever.

"No." I glance around the room before saying, "I'm done."

"Can I still make you dinner? You normally do the cooking, and I want to contribute. I don't want to be a burden." Her eyes drop to the floor, where there are more cracks in the tiles than in my silent contemplation.

"Look at me, Delaina." I tip her chin up with the crook of my finger and see more tears in her big brown depths. Yet, she isn't sobbing like she did before.

"I'm sorry." Her soft apology has so much depth that my heart aches for her.

"Why say sorry? I don't mind if you cook." I yearn to lean in and take her mouth, sweep my tongue inside and taste her. But I don't. Instead, I step back, dropping my hand and put the broom back in the small cabinet. "So, what's on the menu?"

Her eyes widen with small amazement. Then a tiny smile inches across her face. "I could still make pasta, but I want to use actual tomatoes and other ingredients I've seen in the back room."

"So, no jar sauce then?" I joke.

Her smile drops, before glancing at the last few jars on the counter. "I can use—"

"You use whatever you want," I interject with a chuckle. "As long as I don't have to cook, sounds good to me," I then head out of the back room.

"Then give me an hour or so, and I'll have dinner ready. You won't mind if I use the fireplace?" Joy fuses in her words, before Delaina grabs two pots and carries them to the stove.

"Not at all. My aunt used it for cooking all the time." It's the first real chance to talk about her. I drop on the couch, next to Treg and watch the woman rush about. "She loved to cook like that."

Delaina shrugs. "I think I will, too." She then takes the smaller pot to the sink and fills it halfway with water. I don't know what she means by that, but I like the sound of it.

From the back room, she takes several tomatoes that I bought from the farmer's market in town a couple of days ago and proceeds to clean them.

The woman's a natural in the kitchen... as long as she's not destroying things in the process.

Once the tomatoes are destemmed and washed, she places them in a fireproof pan, and proceeds to drizzle olive oil over them. Delaina then places the pan in the fireplace where the flames are at its peak.

It doesn't take long for the aromatic scent to saturate the air, which has my stomach growling.

Delaina skins a small onion, a couple of garlic cloves and tosses them in the deep pan. As she moves around my kitchen while humming out a tune. I'm not familiar with the song, and I'm suddenly hungrier, but not for food.

My eyes follow her luscious ass, as she sways to the beat with the song she's quietly singing. Delaina's dancing about, totally forgetting that I'm here watching her. Her lips tick up into a smile so genuine that my breath catches, and I'm smiling along with her.

For the first time in a very long time, this house feels like a home again. Not a shell of a place that Aunt Winnie left me in her will after she died. I don't feel so alone either, which suddenly draws my attention to that point.

I like being alone. But am I lonely?

My thoughts are interrupted by Delaina calling Treg over. My dog jumps down from the couch, tail wagging as he heads toward her while she tosses a carrot into the air. Treg doesn't hesitate and snatches the orange vegetable in mid-air. After chomping on a few more baby carrots, he trundles his hairy ass back to me and drops down on his belly.

Not wanting to sit there like a dumb stump, I get up and set the small table with the special plates Aunt Winnie used to set out when we had guests show up for dinner. Then I grab the utensils, paper napkins, and glasses, for wine I also picked up from the market.

"Those are pretty," she chirps, staring down at my aunt's plates. I'm glad she likes the red and yellow rose pattern.

"They were Aunt Winnie's."

"Oh. Then I'll be careful with them." She gently places the bowl full of pasta down, along with the loaf of crusty bread on the table. "I hope you're hungry."

A paw on my leg has me looking down at my dog. "Begging isn't you." I push him off and retrieve a treat for Treg.

Once he takes off with his boon, Delaina and I sit at the table. We quietly pass the food to each other and begin eating without a sound from either of us. Not sure when the awkward flooded back into the room, but I miss her humming.

"Do you normally cook like this?" I aim for amiable, but it doesn't sit well with me. I'm not an amiable guy, but for Delaina, I'm trying.

"Hardly." She chuckles and glances down at her plate. "Tell me about your aunt."

13

D^{elaina}

MERRICK'S HAND pauses in midair. A piece of angel hair pasta dangles between the tines of the fork. His eyes reach mine, and he straightens in the seat.

"I'm sorry for asking. I thought since you brought her up, you don't mind talking about her. But if she's a—"

"No. I don't mind talking about Aunt Winnie." Merrick puts down his fork, scoops up his wine glass and swallows a healthy dose, like he needs the liquid courage.

I sit there, quiet, while continuing to eat slowly. I don't want to push, but I sense this Aunt Winnie is a sensitive subject. I'm about to tell him not to worry, when Merrick begins talking.

"I don't remember my father. I think he was never in

the picture. But it was always my mom and me." He blows a heavy breath and continues. "Until it wasn't."

Don't ask me why, but I drop my fork and reach out and take his hand. "I'm sorry."

Merrick shakes his head, but he doesn't release my hand. "It was a long time ago."

"How old were you when she..." I can only assume his mother died, but I'm not sure if I should press further.

"I was seven. She decided that she didn't want to be a mother and left me for a man." I could feel heat rise from my chest to my neck at my sudden indignation on Merrick's behalf. "He didn't want kids, so she dropped me off at a hospital in Pittsburg and took off."

"Jesus," I utter, not able to fathom a mother would do something like that to her own kid. But I'm not ignorant to the world around us. Even parents are terrible to their children. "How did you find that out?"

Merrick releases my hand and stands. "She told me as she dropped me off in front of the emergency entrance. But karma was on my side, if that is what you want to call it."

He's so still, that I'm afraid to breathe or he'd take off on me again.

But I can't seem to shut my mouth for nothing. "I don't understand," I say, meeting his eyes that pierces straight through me.

"Soon after my mother left me, she got into a car accident with a truck, and died instantly," he explains, and begins pacing. "An ER nurse found me standing outside. She took me in, had a doctor check me out, all the while asking me questions. Don't know how long I was there, but the EMTs wheeled in gurneys. One had my mother on it."

I gulp down the knot at the back of my throat, understanding now how he found out about the accident. I don't ask anything else. But Merrick isn't done.

"I heard the nurses and doctors talking—one of the EMTs announced her name—and I knew what had happened. And that she died. So, for most of my childhood I was in the foster system. In and out of different homes. Bad situations to worse. But I survived those worse times."

The tickle at the back of my throat turns into a full-blown ache. My eyes are stinging as they well up with tears.

I don't realize that Merrick is kneeling in front of me, his gentle fingers wiping the wetness off my cheek. "Don't cry for me. I'm here, and whole, because of Aunt Winnie."

"How did she find you?"

"That's kind of a funny story. Aunt Winnie got a DNA testing kit from one her friends. She told me that she wasn't going to do it, but her friend had insisted. So to shut her friend up, she swabbed her mouth and sent it in. I was sixteen by then, and since I was in the system, the company pinged me." Merrick stands, gets back in his chair and snags his fork up.

"Therefore, she reached out to you?" I also resume my eating, but I don't feel hungry anymore.

"Once she found out who I was, she made a call to her lawyer friend, and through him, Great Aunt Winnie adopted me. She was my mom's mother's sister. If you wanted to know."

The tension in my chest recedes that I know Merrick had found his family. "Got it. But what happened next?"

Merrick huffs out a laugh. "I thought it was a joke. Until the CWS social worker drove me here, and I met Aunt Winnie. She was the mirror image of my mother, but twice as old."

His exuberance about his aunt kept growing with each story. Merrick talked well into the night about his antics, and all the crappy things he did, until he learned to trust and love.

"I loved that old woman. But I needed more than just this land. More than the love she openly gave me without asking for anything back. Don't get me wrong, even at sixteen and seventeen, she took out the switch to my ass... When she caught me off guard, of course, which was more times than not." Merrick rubs at his face with both hands. "I did love that woman, but I didn't say it enough. And when I left for the Marines, I knew I broke her heart. However, at the end of every letter Winnie sent me, she wrote that she still loved me and told me not to die."

I bust out a laugh. "Really?"

"Yeah," he chuckles and lets out a breath that sounds more like relief. "She was the one who taught me about life, unconditional love, and trust." His jovialness is gone and replaced with a serious undertone I can't ignore.

"How did you get into the killer for hire line of work?" Maybe that's the wrong question to ask him, but we are this far into the rabbit hole of his life, so I ask it.

"That's for another day."

Cue. Don't ask.

"Okay," I say, and look down at my plate. But something inside me needs answers. "Why didn't you kill me when you had the chance?"

Merrick's body locks up in place. He's so still, I swear he could be a statue. "It doesn't matter. I just didn't."

"Yes, it does. It matters to me. Please tell me the truth. I deserve that." I point to my chest. Not for sorrow for a boy whose mother left him, but for me, who has nobody but a hitman that didn't pull the trigger. "Tell me."

Merrick swings around and faces me. "Do want to hear that my dick got hard when I first saw you? Do want to hear that I wanted to fuck you until you couldn't stand on your own and I'd still wanted to fuck you? Do you want to hear that for the first time in my life, I had no control over my cock?"

Merrick's face goes splotchy, and his glare is like ice, before he strides away without another word.

I don't know what comes over me, but I shout out, "Sure, go run and hide in your room—like you always do, and not talk to me. At least your dick likes me." I cover my mouth with both hands at the last dig.

Why did I say that? After all the wonderful food, the talk about Aunt Winnie, and how Merrick opened up about his mother. I'm such a bitch.

14

M errick

Jesus fucking Christ. Don't look at her. Just keep on walking, if you know what's good for you.

It's taking everything in me not to turn around, bend Delaina over my knee and spank her bratty ass. I know she's afraid and out of her element. I also know she's worried that I'll go back on my word and kill her—but fuck, doesn't she understand who she's dealing with? Or what's out there in the real world?

Apparently not, as I can still hear her yelling from the entryway of the house. I promptly slam the bedroom door to block out her words and anchor myself in the quiet of the space, but I can't help smirking at her vitriol.

Glancing at my private space, I feel somewhat calm. The small bedroom is sparsely furnished, but it's enough for me. There's a full-size bed, a single nightstand, a tall dresser, and a square table for cleaning my guns. Perfect.

With blatant focus, I begin clearing off said table to prep my rifle. One thing the military taught me was to keep my weapons in working order. And to do that, I have to break them down, make sure each part is cleaned and oiled.

I retrieve my gun box from the bed, remove Katie from her case, and lay my rifle on the stand. From the removal of the cheek piece to the bolt, I begin breaking it down.

Focus and clean your weapon, I keep telling myself.

Not sure how long I've been sitting there, but when I look up, Delaina's standing in the doorway watching me. How in the hell did she get into my room. The door is locked... or was it?

"How did you get in here?" Our eyes meet, and a heap of indignation snaps between us.

"The door was unlocked," she says with annoyance.

"What do you want?" I growl back. She's in my house, and I'm protecting her. I don't deserve her anger.

She winces at my cutting question, drops her eyes and turns away. "Um... I'm sorry..."

A giant-sized fist of guilt slams into my gut. Feeling like a total prick for lashing out at her, I throw down the dirty, greasy t-shirt I use to clean my gun and go after her.

"Wait, Delaina." I trail her to the living room, where I reach for her arm. "Stop. Talk to me."

"There's nothing to say, Merrick. Go back to cleaning

your gun." She pulls out of my hold. "I'm going to go for a walk."

"But—"

Delaina steps back, out of my reach and shakes her head. "No, Merrick. You made it clear that you want to be alone. I won't bother you anymore. I'll be my own company—heck, I'll take your dog with me—talk to Treg —which, by the way is a stupid name. I want to change it."

Jesus H. Christ. Delaina won't shut up. She is so fucking frustrating, combative, and stubborn to the point that she's driving me crazy. Even Treg's whining, as he takes off through the doggy door.

I know how to shut her up and get her full attention. I snag her hand, yank her to me until we're chest to chest. The yearning to have her under me overpowers any will I have left to keep away from her.

"If you won't listen to my words, then you will listen to this." Then I kiss her. All lips and tongue, I devour her mouth like she's my last meal on this earth.

For a brief moment, Delaina struggles against me. Then her body goes pliant and molds into me like she's my missing puzzle piece.

With a husky moan, her fingers rake through my hair and one leg wraps around my waist. I cup her ass and grind my rigid dick against her sex.

I nip at her lower lip. "I so need to fuck you, Delaina."

"I so want you to fuck me, Merrick."

I pour my lust into our kiss, before Delaina pulls back and works on my belt and the button on my jeans. Her determination only amps up my need to be inside this woman.

She pulls down my jeans and boxers until my erect cock is free. She then wraps her fingers around the shaft and strokes. I grunt at the pleasure as her talented hands work my dick until precum dribbles out from the tip.

Delaina dips down, her sweet mouth captures my sensitive head, and she sucks back the milky fluid. A moan escapes from my lips as pleasure rushes to my balls.

Desperate to be deep inside her, I pull Delaina up, and our mouths collide with hungry abandon. My hands frantically strip off her clothes until she's fully naked. Lifting her in my arms, we fall onto the large sofa.

This sofa has to be older than me. It's creaking from our weight, but my sole attention is on Delaina and her luscious body.

"Merrick," she says my name like a taunt. My dick's desperate to be between her thighs, but I want to taste her wet heat.

From her mouth, I skim my lips down her neck to her beautiful breasts, cupping each mound. I suck each tight tempting bud into my mouth, savoring her body. She arches up, giving me more access her to rosy peaks. I take advantage and suckle harder until she cries out with desire.

I then trail down her torso, spreading her legs apart, until I see the slick folds awaiting me. I unintentionally lick my lips before leaning in and running the tip of my tongue down her tender flesh.

"Merrick, I don't want foreplay. Just fuck me already," she croons out, her fingers digging into my scalp.

No foreplay? Fine by me.

With a little of her honeyed taste on my tongue, I stretch on top of her and kiss her again. Delaina's legs wrap around my waist, and her pelvis arches up to meet my downward grind.

"Hurry," she demands breathlessly against my mouth, her teeth nipping my lower lip.

"I need a condom," I say, pulling away and reaching for my pants. I grab my wallet and retrieve the only condom inside there, hoping it's not too old. Delaina drops her legs, and I move to my knees and quickly roll on the latex. Without hesitation, I slowly sink into her slippery folds.

"Heck, yes." Delaina arches her back, her pert dark nipples on display like a delicacy to be had.

I slowly pull out and watch as I slide my cock back in. With a growl of pure pleasure, I thrust again and again. Slowly, evenly, until I'm buried to the hilt in her sweet heat.

Christ, it has been a long time since I last had sex— even longer for great sex. And right now, this doesn't compare to anyone else I've stuck my dick in—no. This is nothing like any feeling I've had with anyone before.

Delaina's much more.

Lifting her right leg over my shoulder, I spread her other leg wider, then thrust deeper and faster into her until she croons out my name. I like that, too.

But it's not enough to just be inside this woman. I want to own her in every way so that she'll never forget me, and her body will only desire my touch.

I pull out and lift Delaina until she's facing away from

me. "Hands on the back of the couch, your knees to the cushions. Spread wide for me. I want to see everything."

Her eyes go from glimmering lust to absolute fire at what I'm demanding, and she does my bidding.

"Ass out, sweetheart," I order with a quick slap to her ass cheek.

A low hiss leaves her lips, but she complies with a devilish smile cresting her face.

"Yes. That's it—Jesus, baby. Your pussy is dripping for me." I run a finger between her cleft before positioning my dick at her entrance. Wanting to savor every moment, I leisurely feed in my meaty length. She tries to push back, but I grip onto her hips, stalling her action. "Don't move."

She releases another moan as I push in my cockhead. With one hand now on her shoulder, I slide my other hand between her legs and stroke her clit with my fingers. She shudders with pleasure.

"Do you like that baby?" I then drive in to the hilt.

"Fuck. Yes," Delaina groans, spreading her thighs even wider. She tips her hips, which has my cock going deeper inside her. "Mer—"

It's all she gets out before I pull out and slam back in, over and over until she matches the rhythm of my thrusts. She's as ravenous and eager as I am. As I speed up my thrusts, she clamps hard around my cock and that familiar electric charge surges at the base of my spine and goes right to my nuts.

"Fucking hell—Delaina, come for me," I demand as I fuck her even harder.

Her entire body draws tight, and a keening moan

expels from her as our bodies slam together and we ride out our orgasms.

Delaina collapses against the sofa, and all the while her pussy's taking all the cum from my balls. I fold over her, my forehead on the back of her neck, breathing in our mixed scent. With my dick still deep inside her, I know I have to get rid of the filled condom soon.

Once my heart eases back into a normal rhythm, I pull out and see the broken latex. I freeze as I watch my seed seep out of Delaina.

My mind begins spinning out of control from the possible result of my fuck up. I shouldn't have used the condom.

Fuck... What was I thinking?

I shouldn't have slept with Delaina, especially knowing the fucking condom was older than Aunt Winnie. Still, I don't want kids, certainly don't want to be tied down by anyone. Even worse? I don't know how she's going to react once she finds out the latex broke. Will she blame me?

15

D elaina

Merrick abruptly stands behind me, tense and quiet.

"What's wrong?" I ask, looking over my shoulder, and catching his freaked-out look. His wide, crazed eyes aren't on my face. No. They're lower. Then I feel it. The wetness on the inside of my thighs. Dripping... "Shit. Don't tell me."

Then he meets my eyes with a wary flinch. "I didn't..."

Should I be angry? I think about it for three seconds and immediately decide I'm not. Merrick did put on a condom. And it wasn't his fault that the damn thing broke.

Even under the sex-induced brain fog, I should tell him I'm on the pill.

Though as I watch the panic filter across his face, I

wonder for a brief moment if I should make him squirm for a while? I mean he does deserve a little payback for the way he talked to me earlier. Yet, it's not fair to Merrick to have him think I can get pregnant. That's a bitch thing to do. And I'm not a bitch.

Before I can tell him, Merrick stalks away, leaving me in the living room alone, and naked with his semen dripping down my leg.

"Merrick," I call out his name, but he doesn't respond. Quickly picking up my clothes—and his, I head upstairs and face his closed bedroom door. The same room I found him in not thirty minutes ago. I try the door, but it's locked again. "Merrick," I call out, and knock. But there's no answer.

Since I don't want to stand out here with this mess running down my leg, I head to the hall bathroom. I find some towels and start the shower. The hot water feels wonderful against my sore muscles, especially the tender parts between my legs.

Not feeling guilty for using his soap or the shampoo and conditioner on the shelf, I wash up and then climb out of the tub to dry off.

With the towel wrapped tightly around me, I step out into the hall and catch the sound of a car door slamming.

"What the..." I race downstairs and out the front door, only in a towel, for the whole world to see. "Merrick," I scream at the giant jerk for taking off in the minivan and leaving me alone in an unfamiliar place. He doesn't even bother to let Treg stay.

I swallow down the tightness in my throat before a

shiver overtakes my body. I'm not sure if it's from the cool wind of the coming night or if it's that Merrick has deserted me here.

This is all your fault.

Damn it. I should have told him right away that I'm on the pill. But he took off without talking to me. Who does that?

Now, here I am, alone in a place I don't know. With fear trickling into my veins, I rush back inside the house and lock the front door. I head back upstairs, turn on the lights in the living room and spot my duffle bag on the beautiful wooden bench. Running a hand over the picturesque scene carved into the backrest, I once again admire the detailed work as I try to calm my panic.

"I wonder whose handiwork this is." It doesn't matter. I swipe away a rogue tear, snatch up my bag and head upstairs to dress in a pair of black yoga pants and a black t-shirt that reads, *Girls can do anything,* in hot pink lettering.

As my mind replays our dinner and Merrick's revelations about his Aunt Winnie, guilt filters in, but not enough to be earnest. Especially since the bastard left me here alone.

My stomach growls and I realize that I actually ate very little of the meal. I'm hungry.

Throwing my still damp hair up in the usual bun on top of my head, I troop back down to the kitchen for something to eat. I open the small refrigerator and see the container of pasta. Instead of the angel hair, I choose a red apple, a package of sliced ham, mustard, and the container of potato salad. On the countertop is the bread bin. I lift the lid and take out the bread leftover from dinner.

Grabbing a plate from one of the upper cabinets, I make a ham sandwich with mustard, plop some salad on the side and cut up the apple. With a bottled water, a plateful of food and a fork in hand, I go into the living room where the large fireplace takes up one stone wall.

Since there's no television, I glance back at the hearth. "Why not," I mutter to myself. I place my food on the rectangular coffee table and stoke the fire, then adding another log, just like how Merrick taught me.

With the ambiance set, I finally sit down on the couch —the same couch where I had the best climax ever. I tuck my legs under me and dig into my food.

When three quarters of the sandwich, half the salad and the apple are finished, I snag the throw that's on the couch and snuggle in. Between a belly full of food and the heat from the fireplace, I fall right to sleep despite the thoughts swirling in my mind that, no matter how much I want to hate Merrick for leaving me alone, I can't.

Who knows how long I was laying on the couch before I felt a cold hand caressing my cheek. The moment I open my eyes, thinking it's Merrick, the hand callously clamps down on my mouth and terror swallows me whole because a masked man is staring down at me.

16

M errick

WHAT THE FUCK is wrong with me? I left Delaina unprotected, just so I can run and not face the reality of what happened between us—let alone the issue with the condom breaking.

I'm also bigger asshole for taking Treg with me. I should have left him home, but I wasn't thinking.

I might be using the excuse of finally returning the minivan, but let's call the kettle black, like Aunt Winnie used to say. I'm a fucking coward, and I didn't even stop to ask her if she was on birth control before I shoved my cock inside her. No, I just fucked her like a horn dog and didn't bother making sure was she okay.

What's worse? Add the imminent problem we're facing, and this entire situation is a damn shitshow.

Bottom line, I'm far from being a good man. I'm a killer. There's no way of wiping the blood stains from my past actions. But this? I even despise myself.

She's too good for the likes of me. I know it and I hope Delaina understands that truth, once I figure out how to remove the hit, and we go our separate ways. In the meantime, I hope she forgives me for leaving her alone.

After dropping off the rental, I walk one mile to where I left my truck, climb in and head home. Passing a drug store, the idea of buying condoms pops into my head. I hesitate for only a second, before I turn the vehicle around and park. This might be futile getting the condoms, because Delaina probably doesn't want anything to do with me now.

"Better safe than sorry, boy." Aunt Winnie words play in my head.

Once I get back on the road, I think about calling Delaina. But I realize she doesn't have a cell phone, since she dropped the damn thing into the water. And the house's landline was disconnected soon after Aunt Winnie died. So there's no way of getting ahold of her and vice versa.

Halfway home, as the dusk fades to dark, my insides are a gnarled ball of dread, and the need to get back becomes an urgency. I drive as fast as possible until I'm a mile from the house. Knowing this terrain like the back of my hand, I shut off the headlights but keep a steady speed. Something was telling me to be wary.

This ill feeling might be nothing, but I always follow my gut. Treg begins to whine as though he's reacting to the tension in the air. With Delaina's life on the line, I have to pull my head out of my ass and be more vigilant than ever.

Not a second after I round the hill, I stop, and put the truck into park. Under an ebony sky filled with stars, I see the front door wide open and the orange glow from within the house sparks to a brighter radiance. A gutting ache pierces my chest at the thought of Delaina hurt or worse.

"Shit. Delaina."

Pulling my spare Ruger from the glove compartment, along with an extra clip, I open the door and let Treg jump out. He immediately bolts straight for the house, with me a few yards behind while keeping an ear open for any sound.

Treg waits by the open door, where I give his collar a tug before letting him go. Normally he would ferret out anyone inside the house. Instead, he bolts up the stairs.

A prickle of unease rushes over me as I follow him. Treg's jumping and barking at the closed bathroom door.

Every muscle in my body draws tighter against my bones, with each cautious step down the hallway. After hastily checking the two bedrooms to my right, I reach the closed bathroom door.

Not wanting Treg to run inside, I pull at his collar and motion for my dog to heel. He follows my orders, albeit with a soft whine.

Checking the door, I find it locked. I kick it, the wood splinters, and the door swings open and crashes against the wall. In the bathtub, filling with water, Delaina is out cold, and trussed up like a roped calf. She has a bloody lip and a swollen right eye.

The moment I hurry inside, Treg growls. I spin around

and find my dog's on a masked intruder. Without thinking, I aim for his head and pull the trigger, but he jerks around, and the bullet hits him in the left shoulder.

He grunts but continues wrestling his arm out of Treg's iron jaws. Then the fucker punches the side of Treg's head, momentarily knocking the dog out.

The son of a bitch takes off toward the stairs, and I rush into the hallway, take aim and shoot. Before he reaches the staircase, my bullet nails his left knee. He screams out in agony and then tumbles down the stairs with rapid thuds.

Knowing the bastard won't go far, I quickly check Treg, who's shaking off the attack. Knowing he's good, I race back into the bathroom. I turn off the faucet and pull Delaina out of the tub.

After laying her on the floor, I cut her bonds. Then I put two fingers to her neck, and a deluge of relief washes over me when I felt her pulse.

Now that Delaina's safe, especially with Treg by her side, I'm going after the motherfucker who infiltrated my home.

"Stay," I command Treg.

Following the blood smears down the steps, the trail leads out of the house. The bastard won't be far—not with two bullet wounds that are bleeding out.

Even under the dark sky, I know my land intimately. So it doesn't take me long to find the guy's mask and more blood coming up on the next ridge.

I see you in my sights, asshole.

He's easy prey, sprawled out in the tall grass with a shattered knee, laying limp and bloody. With my gun aimed at his head, I take out the small flashlight from my back pocket and point to his face. He has the same color hair as the other three and similar facial features. This one has to be Mable's too.

"Don't move a muscle." I want nothing more than to pull out my knife and cut this fucker up from limb to limb, for what he did to Delaina. However, I need answers and he's going to give them to me.

The dumbass raises a hand, then drops it. "Where the hell do you think I'm going, asshole?" Agony cuts across his face.

I chuckle. "Nowhere, now." I bend a knee and study the doughy shape of his body. He's not made for this type of work. I can tell a hitter from a desk jockey.

I point the gun to his foot. "Tell me, how did you find me? And don't bother telling me you have a partner around here. I know you're working alone. I shoot one toe off at a time until I get the truth out of you." It's a ruse but the dick doesn't need to know that.

"Fuck you," he spits out and groans.

"You're not my type." I aim the flashlight at his face, blinding him. "You're one of Mable's boys."

His eyes go wide. Yep. I hit the mark.

"How many of you are left—Wait—Don't answer that. Better yet, call your mother. We need to have a chat," I say evenly.

"She won't talk to you," he says with a shudder. His body's shaking from the loss of blood.

"But I think she will, especially if you want to remain breathing," I warn, aiming the gun at his head again.

He stares at me for a long minute before he points to the front pocket of his pants. "My phone is in there."

I point the light at his pants pocket. "Take out the phone slowly—but remember, I'll shoot you dead if you're lying."

"I'm not." With an unsteady hand, he slides the phone out, hits a couple buttons and places it to his ear. "Mamma?... Yeah... No. I'm bleeding bad. Uh, no... Yeah... He's here... Okay." As his eyes train on me, he extends his hand. "She wants to talk to you."

I carefully take the bloody phone and put it close to my ear. "Yes?"

"You son of a bitch," Mable screeches like a banshee.

"Now, is that how you talk to someone, Mable?" *Can I be any more condescending?*

"Listen up, you rotten piece of shit. You killed three of my sons, and now Brady's bleeding out. Normally, I don't negotiate with heartless bastards, but that's my boy you have there." The tight restraints of her voice have me watchful to what is around me and the guy on the ground. I can't relax, knowing how cunning Mable can be.

"Negotiate?" I question with a snort. "Okay, I'm listening."

"I deserve retribution for what you did to my boys," she screams into the phone.

I stay cool but purposeful. "Listen to me loud and clear, because I'm going to say this once. This is business, Mable. I was on my mark when your boys encroached. Rules of the game. I took them out. There's no doubt your boys would have done the same to me if they were in my shoes. Now, since you're on your last son, I suggest you pull out now, withdraw any deals you have on me, and your son can walk away *alive*."

"You're in no position—"

"I see you're not comprehending where I'm standing on this, Mable. Don't mistake keeping your son alive, while I'm talking to you as charity. I can pull the trigger at any time. My lack of ability to give two fucks about your situation is where I'm at. This business is to kill or be killed. And I prefer the first. Now, as for *my mark,* she's mine. And Mable? Let me make it very fucking clear to you. If you don't step the fuck back from me and my mark, you will find yourself and your last son at the end of my barrel and you won't see it coming. Understand?"

Silence.

My eyes land on the bleeding guy on the ground. "Tick tock, Mable. You're losing precious time and your son's losing blood."

"All right. Fuck—I understand."

"Perfect." I hang up and move to the guy's side, where his eyes are at half-mast. He doesn't look good. I slap at his face. "Hey, wake up."

"What?" He blinks rapidly. "You're going to kill me?"

"I should for what you did to Delaina. But no. I won't kill you."

He visibly relaxed, then winces with pain.

Then a thought hit me. "Why didn't you just shoot the woman? Why go through the elaborate plan of drowning her?"

The asshole drops his eyes. "To make it look like a suicide."

"Huh, okay. You can leave now, and don't come back."

"How?" he cries out. "My knee is shattered, and I can't move my arm," he whimpers.

"Not my problem. Now get off my land or I will shoot you where you lie." I walk away, wondering if I'll find him in the same spot, dead, in the morning.

17

Delaina

Cocooned in warmth, I snuggle against steely heat. Sudden pain radiates from my face, and I jerk back. Popping open one eye, I see nothing but a wall of muscled chest. A naked muscled chest, which I swiftly assess is Merrick's.

Then the realization hits me that I'm almost as naked—aside from my panties, and entangled around Merrick's boxer-clad body.

Suddenly remembering that I hate this man, I sit up but then almost fall off the bed while attempting to scramble away from Merrick. Gracefully, he swoops me into his strong arms before I hit the floor with my face.

"Calm," he says soothingly in my ear.

"Calm? You left me alone, you jerk," I argue, pushing

and slapping at his arms to release me. "Wait," I gasp as memory of an intruder skids into my brain. "There was a guy..." I frantically look around. "He surprised me... and punched my face when I wouldn't listen to him." I touch my nose, which feels swollen.

"It's not broken," Merrick says tenderly as he skims a finger down my cheek. "And you don't have to worry about him anymore." That isn't an answer, but at the same time, it's Merrick. I know what he's not saying.

"He was another hitman, wasn't he?"

"Yes." The lazy way he's looking has me instantly on guard. I don't trust myself around him, certainly not when my body erupts with fiery lust. So, I shove his hand off me, get to my feet, and step away from the bed.

"Okay, now what?" I plant my hands on my hips and attempt to look serious despite the lack of clothes.

That devilishly handsome grin has me melting like a popsicle on a hot summer day. Merrick leans back against the headboard, placing one arm behind his head and the other on his abs. I find my eyes following his movements. I attempt to dispel those damn drunken butterflies trying to take flight all at the same time in my belly.

Get it together, Delaina. Remember, he's a killer, not your boyfriend.

Just thinking of those excuses sounds so paltry, especially since I let him fuck me. Yet, there's only one reason why we are here together. He came to kill me. Why do I keep forgetting that bit of information when I'm around him?

I need to get away from here—from Merrick and this

entire shitshow. Maybe I can change my name and the way I look. Yeah—that's what I need to do.

"Whatever's roaming around in your mind, just forget it," Merrick snaps as he sits up, grabs my hand, and tugs me on top of him.

"I don't know what you're talking about—and let go of me," I huff out, not trying too hard to wiggle out of his hold.

He quickly releases me, and I scramble away from him again.

He sits up, his face a mask of seriousness. "We need to talk, Delaina," he says and gently pats the bed next to him. "Please."

I'm taken aback by his plea.

"What, Merrick?" I sit at the edge of the bed, leaving a big gap between us.

"Come closer and kiss me."

I arch a brow. "Why?"

"Because I know you need it." He says this so casually that it takes a second for me to realize what he said.

I straighten, and gawk at the audacity of this man. "Well, aren't you full of yourself."

"I'd rather you be full of me." He grabs me around the middle, pulls me down onto the bed and hovers over me like a hulking force I can't deny.

I laugh, trying to wiggle out of his hold. But Merrick does a move I can't even describe and has me back on the bed, with his body plastered on top of mine.

"Merrick..." It's all I get out before he kisses me. Gentle and sweet. His growing erection nestled between my thighs. The sudden yearning to have him inside me shadows any desire to flee.

"I almost lost you," Merrick admits solemnly. "I will not leave you again."

"You promised me that before," I whisper, desperately needing his touch.

"I promise," he says with a sweltering kiss.

As Merrick grinds his cock into me, his damn cell phone goes off.

"Fuck." He jackknifes off me and retrieves the device from his pants pocket. "What?"

"Who is it?" I mouth to him as he listens to the other person on the line.

"Hold on, Joe." Merrick taps the screen and I hear the other guy loud and clear. "Go ahead."

"I tracked down who put the hit out on your mark," Joe says with nervous splutter, like he drank too many energy drinks and couldn't get the words out fast enough.

"Her name is Delaina. Use it," Merrick growls.

"Delaina. Right. Anyway, it took a bit since this old system is slower than frickin' molasses. But I found the account where it originated from."

"And?" Merrick's impatience mimics mine.

"The contract was from Brent Miller."

"Why am I not surprised?" Merrick grit out through clenched teeth.

The blow of shock at hearing my stepfather's name hits me square in the chest.

"There's more," Joe adds with expelled breath.

"Go on," Merrick says, but his attention is on the floor.

The vomit's rising up to my throat, and I'm choking with fear of what Joe is going to say next.

"The mark—I'm mean Delaina's stepbrother Mark Miller also took out a contract for a *grab and scare*—which by the way is a stupid name."

"What's that?" I ask, tasting the acidic burn in my mouth.

Merrick's eyes train on mine. "It's what that guy in Florida tried to do."

"And the scare part?" I ask, as the tears well up.

"Different means of torture," Joe announces, his words oddly muffled.

"Joe," Merrick hisses.

"I'm going to be sick." I run out of the bedroom and make it to the toilet, where I retch up everything in my stomach.

This entire time Brent wanted me dead and Mark wanted me tortured. And for what? The pain at that admission hurts worse than the punch to the face my step-brother had given me.

I don't know what I did to deserve this, but all I want to do is crawl in a hole and hide from the world.

18

M errick

"WHAT DO you want me to do?" Joe asks as I follow Delaina to the bathroom.

"Nothing right now."

"So I'm guessing the million is vapors?" Joe asks with resolve.

"Like a fucking ghost." Then I hang up.

The rage inside me splits in half as I watch Delaina over the toilet bowl, retching her guts out.

I bend a knee and rub a gentle hand on her back—but fuck—seeing her so vulnerable only adds to my rising need to protect her from this shitty world. From the people who have done nothing but hurt her. I want to track down both her step-assholes and put a bullet between their eyes.

I knew deep down in my core—from the very beginning, my gut told me it's between the stepfather or step-brother. But it doesn't matter, because they both are going to die.

Delaina sits back, her head banging slightly against the wall. I grab a plastic cup of water and a wet washcloth, and hand them both to her. She sucks back the water and then wipes her mouth.

"Why me?" she asks as tears rim her eyes and then stream down her red tinged cheeks.

I cram my ass down next to her, take the cup and towel out of her hands and toss them in the sink. "I don't know, Delaina. But if you want to find out why, we will go back to Florida and get those answers."

With wide, watery eyes, she angles her head my way. "Really? You'd come with me?" she asks softly like she's afraid I'd say no.

I lean in, meeting her eye to eye. "Yes."

Something flickers across her face I can't decipher. A hint of her vulnerability falls away and a soft sweet smile appears on her face. Seeing Delaina happy is a foreign concept to me. Fucking strange, to be precise.

Before I started this contract, I didn't give a shit one way or another about a mark. But this time I do. And I can't deny the peace Delaina gives me here, in my private space. In my dreary life.

Delaina surprises me and climbs onto my lap. She plants a gentle kiss on my lips and then nuzzles her face into the crook of my neck. "Thank you."

"For what?" I wrap my arms around her and inhale the scent in Delaina's hair.

"For not killing me. And for helping me stay alive."

A chuckle bubbles out of me as she presses tighter to my chest. I have to admit I like her there.

"You're welcome," I say, absorbing her goodness. A swirl of want begins to tailspin into a demanding need to be inside this woman. My woman.

She laughs and then pulls back, losing her smile. "So, how do we do this?"

I run a finger along Delaina's jaw, before cupping her face, and drawing her close. "First things first," I whisper against her sweet mouth before capturing her lips with no hesitation.

Delaina doesn't falter and returns my affection with equal measure, while she grinds down on my hard length, making me manic with desire to claim her on every surface in this house.

Making absolutely no apologies for wanting Delaina, especially after what happened to her, I gently grip her hair tight and expose her neck. Feasting on her body is my only goal for now... and making her happy.

I start at her neck, kissing, sucking, and nipping at the tender flesh. Dragging my tongue down to the dip of her collarbone, I graze a hand alongside her left breast. My fingers find her taut nipple and pinch it, which evokes a soft moan from Delaina. I love her sounds, especially when I'm the one who elicits them.

"I don't want to wait, Merrick," she conveys by grinding harder on my cock.

"I promise I'll give it to you good, but I want to taste you. Drown in your scent," I growl and demand, "Stand.

Take off your panties and put your hands on the wall, spread your legs and don't move."

With my demands met, and her pretty pussy at mouth level, I dive in. I swipe my tongue along the seam before I spread her slick lips and suck at her clit. Another groan, much louder this time, croons out of Delaina.

"Merrick," she whispers my name like a prayer as I take a finger and slowly slide inside her. Then two until she's so slick that three fingers can easily slip in deep.

"Sweet and beautiful." Cupping her ass with one hand, I drive my fingers in and out of her. I devour every bit of her tender flesh until she's writhing under me, calling out my name, with the desperate need to cum.

Delaina throws her head back and shouts, "Merrick."

Though she's still on shaky legs, I get up, drop my boxers, and move behind her. "Here's the fucking you wanted, Delaina. Now bend for me." She does my bidding and tips out her hips until she's ass to dick.

After grabbing a condom from the vanity drawer, I quickly roll it on and slide right into Delaina. Her moans match my grunts as I repeatedly thrust inside her tight, wet heat. I fuck her until my balls draw up and her name escapes my lips. She moans out her second release right after me.

We're both panting and tired, but knowing the condom needs to go first, I bend over, kiss the back of her neck, and slide out of her.

I toss the condom in the trash and then scoop Delaina up and carry her to bed. The moment we hit the sheets, she curls into me and falls right to sleep. I lay awake, watching this woman who I've quickly grown feelings for, and marvel at how my life and fate have turned by simply taking this assignment. She may have been my mark for an easy mil when this fiasco started, but now, she's something I can't explain, and I refuse to name what we have.

Once we take care of Brent Miller, then I will reevaluate what's there between us.

"Are you sure you want to do this?" I ask her several hours later.

"No, but do I really have a choice? I want to know why Brent put out a hit for me and what Mark would gain from torturing me. It's not like he hasn't stop tormenting me since I was a kid." Delaina shivers.

Every molecule on my body lights up with fury at Delaina's admission. I want to reach out and console her. But from the way she draws her arms across her chest, tucking back against the headboard and closing her eyes, she wants separation from me.

I don't like it, but I have to give her the space she needs.

A single tear escapes her right eye, but she quickly swipes it away.

We might be in bed, together and naked—aside from the sheet that's partially covering us, but Delaina's a million miles away. Then just as suddenly, she's back in my arms, her mouth on mine.

If she needs sex as an escape, I don't have a problem

giving all that she desires. Anything to wipe the misery from her eyes.

As the night skates away before the coming dawn, I get up to start a fire to ward off the chill in the air, then rejoin Delaina in bed.

I could lay here all day, with the room filled with the scents from our lovemaking and the crackling logs.

I turn on my side, my hand grazes her uncovered leg, draped over my hip. "You know you don't have to do anything. I can take care of them. You'll be clean of all this."

Her eyes pop open, surprise and a hint of ire flash in their dark depths. "I don't want them dead, Merrick. There has been enough blood shed. Besides, they don't deserve a quick death for what they put me through." She shakes her head. "No. I want them to suffer like they've made me suffer. No. They belong in jail for a good long time."

The finality in her voice has me taking in a resolved breath. "Okay, Delaina. We can do it your way. But with this job, comes anonymity. I can't be visibly involved. I hope you understand that. Or my ass will be in jail along with those bastards."

"I understand. I don't want you to get caught either. Even though we met under these terrible circumstances, I want you in my life. But I need to know the why and how from them."

"Then trust me enough to set them up. And Joe will be able to help us with that." I wrap an arm around Delaina and pull her tight against me.

Her warm hand cups my face. "Merrick, I trust you."

My chest tightens and the pressure from a volcano of emotions threatens to spew from my guts at the conviction in her words.

"Delaina." I barely get out her name before I pull her in for a kiss, needing that connection now more than ever. And when she's languorous from all the pleasure I've pulled from her body, then we will set a plan in motion to get rid of the filth that is Brent and Mark Miller.

19

D elaina

It takes another week for Merrick's handler, Joe, to find out more details on my stepfather. I shiver at the thought of the man who—even though I never liked him—had loved my mother.

I've racked my brain as to why Brent wants me dead. It can't be about money or assets, since I don't have any. Unless he wants the land my grandparents bequeathed me. If that's it, he can have the property.

And what of Mark? What could I say about my stepbrother, who to this day has bullied me for years. Damn, I don't want to think about that horrible jerk. Yet, his disappearance doesn't bode well.

"Are you ready?" Merrick asks as he closes and locks the front door to the house I'm going to miss. This last week with Merrick has been magical. We've had sex in practically every room in that home.

We also laughed and enjoyed the simple things like cooking or going for walks along the woodsy trail on the property, like an actual couple. With Treg by our side, one would assume by looking at us, we're in a solid committed relationship.

I only hope, after all is said and done with my stepfather and brother, that Merrick's and my connection will flourish into something stronger.

However, I hate to burst my own bubble. Everything I'm feeling for Merrick isn't real. He's my protector and he cares that I stay alive. But once I'm safe, there's no doubt that we'll go our separate ways and I'll be alone again.

But the sex... I blush at the tsunami of emotions and sensations when I think of Merrick.

"What are you thinking of right now?" Merrick slides on a mischievous grin, which only makes him even more wickedly gorgeous. I wish he would smile more often. He's so much more approachable when he's happy.

"Nothing," I lie, but quickly giggle as his fingers aim for my sides, where I'm most ticklish. He figured that out two nights ago when I was on top of him, reverse cowgirl, and his strong hands glided gently down my sides. I nearly fell off of him from the sudden burst of laughter out of me.

"Not nothing. Tell me," he growls, which has me taking a step back. My heart is racing but for a whole different reason than fear. Excitement and desire shoot through my body as he takes those few steps toward me.

Before I can spin around and take off toward his truck,

Merrick has his arm around my middle and is lifting me up in the air. Treg doesn't want to be left out and jumps up and bumps against Merrick, and he almost drops me.

"Put me down before we both get hurt," I shout out with laughter.

"Give me a kiss and I will," Merrick demands and claims my mouth before I can either protest or give in.

What a difference these last two weeks have made with this man. My hitman. My killer.

Merrick finally puts me back on my feet. With Treg tromping alongside us, we get to the truck and we all climb in. After one final look at the house, we head back down to Florida to hopefully confront Brent and Mark, and find the evidence that will put both of them in jail.

As each mile passes, the trickle of fear gets stronger and it begins to fill me with dread. I trust Merrick whole-heartedly, but what of the other hitmen that are out there? Merrick did say that he made a deal with that woman, but she could have gone back on her word. Merrick's only one man.

I don't know why I doubt his ability to keep me safe. He has proven it time and time again.

"A penny for your thoughts?" Merrick glances at me before returning his attention back to the road.

"Another one of Aunt Winnie's sayings?"

He shrugs. "One of many."

"My head keeps going back to why? I know my stepfather never really cared for me, but in some sense he's never done me harm before this. But Mark, that's another story," I admit.

The air in the truck suddenly shifts from calm to volatile.

"Merrick," I utter calmly, noting the tension in his jaw.

"I want to know exactly what that dickhead did to you," Merrick says through gritted teeth. "Those bruises on that first day we met, they were from him."

"I don't—"

"Don't lie for him, Delaina. I want to know the truth."

Merrick's right. I need to come clean and tell him everything. I slouch back into my seat, look out my window, and wonder where I should start. From the beginning, I guess.

"The day my mother announced to me that she was marrying Brent was the first day I met the man. I was eight at the time. He showed me the typical fatherly moments around my mother, but when Mom turned her back, I saw his true colors. Yet, Mom was happy, and I really didn't mind that my new-to-be stepfather ignored me or criticized me for the littlest things. I quickly learned to ignore him." I glance back at Merrick, who remains silent, but I can still see his jaw working. "Anyway, a week after they got married, Brent announced that his son had decided to move in with us. I didn't think much about it at the time, since he was eighteen and probably heading off to college."

"But you were wrong."

"I was wrong." I expel a tired sigh. "From that first day he came into the house, he cornered me, telling me that no one actually loved me, and he would make sure my life was a living hell. I was eight—almost nine. Who does that shit to a kid?"

"Did you tell your mom?" Merrick asks as he reaches for my hand and squeezes my fingers.

"I did the first few times, but my mom brushed it off, saying I was being dramatic." God, just thinking of those days, I was heartbroken that my mother couldn't see past her own happiness. "After that, I stopped going to her."

"You still haven't told me what that asshole did to you." Merrick's warring glance says more than his words convey.

"It depended on the day. Sometimes, he'd trap me in a room and spout crap, like nobody loved me. Other times, he grabbed me hard and left bruises. There was this one time..." I can't finish, as the flashback of the night of my sixteenth birthday hits me like a runaway train. I realize that if I don't get ahold of myself, I will derail and the fragmented pieces of my life that I've been holding together by sheer willpower will disintegrate and there will be nothing left of me.

"Delaina." His face is inches from mine.

I quickly blink away the tears and realize Merrick has pulled over and parked. He cups my face, lending me the strength I need to tell him. I drop my gaze and stare at the knuckles of my fisted hands turning white as snow.

"Look at me, sweetheart," he whispers. Merrick's warm hand is on my jaw. His thumb is wiping away the wetness on my cheeks. His closeness gives me a modicum of comfort to tell him everything. "Baby, look at me."

I finally meet his eyes and immediately crumble in his arms. The heavy tears I've been holding back for years are now seeping out of my eyes and my fingers clutch at Merrick's t-shirt like a lifeline. "I'm afraid."

"Tell me," he gently insists with a soft kiss to my hair. "What did he do?"

Fear of the long-buried memories of what happened to me all those years ago has me mute. But I can't hold it in any longer. "He bought me a necklace for my sixteenth birthday, but I refused to take it. He got mad and..."

"And?" His voice is drawn tight like a bow string.

"Mark raped me."

20

Merrick

RAPE.

From the moment Delaina confessed what her stepbrother had done to her at sixteen, my rage has demanded a target and Mark is the bullseye.

Every painful tear that seeped out of Delaina only added to the rising inferno of revulsion for the bastard. With every state we pass through, my mind runs a gambit on how I'm going to torture and then kill this fucker.

Just outside of Scranton, Pennsylvania, Delaina turns to me as she pets Treg's neck. "I'm getting a headache, Merrick. Can we stop somewhere and get something to eat?"

"Sure. There's a diner coming up that has decent food."

"Great. Anything will be better than an empty stomach," she utters, then takes a swig of water.

What I want is to stop the truck, scoop her up in my arms, and give her the comfort she needs. Instead, I exit the off ramp to the diner.

Chickie's Diner is about half a mile from downtown Scranton. "It's nothing to look at, but it does have good food and a clean bathroom. And nearly everything on the menu is some sort of chicken dish. So you can't go wrong in choosing what to eat. Unless you don't like chicken."

Delaina finally gives me a smile. The first one, since she told me about the rape.

Since the diner doesn't allow dogs, I take Treg for a quick walk and piss, before locking him in the truck. Then Delaina and I head inside. We take the booth by the window so I can keep an eye on the truck.

"What'll it be?" our waitress, named Tanya, asks, as she smacks her neon pink lips and grins down at us.

With her nose in the menu, Delaina points to an image on the inside fold. "I'll have the soup and sandwich combo. Chicken noodle, the Nantucket chicken salad sandwich, and a cola, please."

"That sounds good. Make that two," I say and pass the menus to our waitress.

"You got it, cutie," Tanya says to me with a wink.

I glance at Delaina to see her reaction, but her attention is out the window.

Reaching for her hand, I pull her focus to me. "What are you thinking about?"

She meets my eyes with wariness. "What would you have done if you were in my shoes?"

"What do you mean?" I ask cautiously, understanding where she's come from.

"If I'd just accepted the necklace. Maybe..." Delaina shakes her head, her eyes downcast to the wooden table. They're brimming with tears. "I feel so... dirty."

Those four words are barely a whisper, but I hear her pain as though she'd screamed it out.

I tighten my grip on her hand. "Listen to me, Delaina Wells. What happened to you wasn't your fault. That bastard took advantage of you. He used your fears. You were only a kid, for Christ sakes. He was the adult. Do you see who's in the wrong here?"

She swallows hard, nods, but doesn't say anything. "I know."

"You were never dirty, sweetheart. Far from it. And, I'll prove it to you every day until you believe it," I vow with everything in me.

"Here are your drinks... Oh honey, you're too pretty to cry," Tanya says, placing the glasses in front of us. She spears me with a glare before turning back to Delaina. "Here's some napkins. If you need the ladies room, it's right over there, sweetie." She points to the other side of the diner, then walks away with one more parting sneer to me.

I'm not bothered. Actually, it's nice to see someone else sticking up for her.

"I'm sorry." Delaina picks up a napkin and blows her

nose. "I'll make sure to tell her that it wasn't you that made me cry."

"I don't give a fuck what she thinks. Let's just eat, then we can let Treg out for a little stretch before we take off. Okay?" I post a smile I'm not feeling, but for Delaina, I'd do anything to ease her burdens.

She blows her nose. "Okay. But I think I need to use the bathroom."

Delaina gets up and heads in the direction where the waitress had pointed. No sooner she's out of my sight, I track a guy, normal and nondescript, getting up from a booth and heading toward the bathroom.

Every one of my instincts is telling me that he's a killer. I get up from the table, and follow, lagging behind him as though I have all the time in the world. I won't pull out my gun, in case there are witnesses.

As he reaches for the woman's bathroom door, I see the back door of the restaurant is wide open, with no obstructions. Without hesitation, I barrel into the fucker until we're outside, not giving him time to reach for his gun.

That's easy enough, but I don't slack on my hold around his middle until I have him on the ground. He fights me at every step. Then a solid punch lands on the side of my head, but I'm a Pitbull, I won't let go.

Once we're a good distance away from the building, I release him, drop and quickly swing out my leg, knocking him on his back.

In that second, we both grab our guns and aim them at each other.

"Who sent you?" I say coolly.

"Does it matter? You and the bitch will be dead." The calculating smile on his face is all the answer I need.

"Mable," I say evenly.

His smile drops, and his eyes shift to what's behind me. But I don't dare look, or breathe.

The barrel of his silencer moves a hair, and I pull the trigger, my aim true. Right between the eyes.

I take a moment before I turn around and find myself standing there alone. Either Delaina took off or this asshole was bluffing. I hope for the latter.

As I turn around, I scan the building for any surveillance cameras. I'm relieved to find none, and walk back inside, to the table, where I see Delaina sitting there drinking coffee. But the look of despair in her eyes says it all.

She saw me kill a man in cold blood.

Even though I did it to keep her safe, I still see trepidation back in her eyes, like when we first met.

We both eat in silence, me keeping my thoughts to myself, and I'm assuming she's doing the same. After we're done, I take Treg for a good walk while Delaina stays in the car. Her excuse is that she's tired.

As much as I need to know where her head's at, again, I give her the space. But an hour past Lancaster, I've finally had enough of her quiet. "Talk to me," I urge while reaching for her hand.

Delaina moves her left hand out of my reach, while her attention is out the window. "I don't know what to say, Merrick—or to think."

"Think of what?"

"I know you have killed, but seeing it firsthand..." she shakes her head. "It's shocking."

I don't want to be angry, but I am. Everything I've done the second she entered my life, I've done for her. "It's not like I was looking for it."

"You could have let him go—"

"So, he could come back and shoot me in the back of the head and yours? Fuck no," I say without remorse.

"How did you know he's a hitman?" *Jesus, is she actually defending the fucker?*

"He tracked us to the restaurant and waited. When you went to the bathroom, he got up and before he went inside to *kill you*, I took him out—You know what? I'm not going to justify my actions to you, Delaina. This is who I am. If you can't handle it. Then I'm sorry."

There's a hitch in her breathing. I turn to see big fat tears trailing down her cheeks. "What did I do to deserve all this, Merrick?" Treg whines, as Delaina breaks down.

I pull over, put the truck into park and wrapped her in my arms the best I can. "You did nothing wrong. There are just too many fucked up people in this world—including me."

"And why does my family want me dead? I never did anything to Brent."

"He's not your family, Delaina. They aren't your blood. Remember that," I say as I pull away and wipe a loose tear from her cheek. "Are you okay?"

"I'm sorry for freaking out." Treg's head pokes between her and I, and he begins licking her face. "I'm sorry, boy for worrying you too."

"Stop saying you're sorry." I huff out before straightening in my seat and putting the truck into gear.

I get back on the road, merge onto Route 30 and then 83, driving toward Glen Burnie, Maryland, making sure no one is following us this time.

"You know, Brent raised me, especially after my mother died. He didn't have to."

"He also let his son rape you under his fucking roof." The second those words spill from my lips, Delaina flinches away and turns her face toward the window.

Well fuck. From the way her shoulders are drawn tight, I cut her deep. Christ, I have a habit of doing that to her.

"I'm sorry. I didn't mean—"

"Yes, you did." She angles her chin my way. "And you're right. I should have told Brent what Mark did to me."

"Yeah. But I shouldn't have been a dick about it and thrown it back at you like that." I regret admitting my thoughts aloud, but the amount of abuse Delaina had dealt with is ridiculously appalling. And I can't believe that Brent was blinded to what his son had done to her.

"I guess that's another question for Brent." She cast a weak smile before leaning her seat all the way back and closing her eyes. "I'm going to take a nap."

"Here." I reach around for a small pillow in the back seat. "This might be more comfortable."

She takes it, tucks the pillow behind her head and closes her eyes. "Thank you, Merrick."

Treg tucks his head next to Delaina's, and falls asleep.

I wait a good twenty minutes until I know for sure

Delaina is asleep, before I pull over and quietly get out of the car. I walk to the back of the truck and dial Joe.

"What's going on boss man?" Joe chirps.

"Did you get a location on Brent?"

"Yeah, but I found some stuff in his finances that's strange."

"What is it?"

"The man's in debt—like up to his eyeballs," Joe says with clicks of a keyboard. "He hardly has a hundred K in his accounts."

"Maybe the million is set aside—"

"No, Merrick. The man's barely holding water with his dealerships. The Sarasota and Orlando branches are about to be closed and the one in Miami is barely floating."

"Is that the one his son works at?"

"Now he does since the Orlando brand is closing. But the funny thing is, Mark has loads in multiple accounts," Joe says with a whistle. "A lot of money."

"What are you saying?"

"I'm saying, Mark has been siphoning profits from his daddy's businesses for a long time and putting it all in his own pocket."

"Without Brent knowing about it? That doesn't make sense," I admit, wondering how stupid Brent actually is.

"Brent's obviously oblivious since he has been trusting Mark to handle all the finances for the last few years. Also, I followed the tiny money thread from where the initial contract was set up, and I found a bank account in Raleigh, North Carolina."

"The name on that account?"

"Are you ready for it? There are several names. But the original person that opened the account was Belinda Miller," Joe says with a click.

"That's..."

"Yep, the mark's mother," he confirms with another few clicks in the background. "And do you know how much is in that account?"

"Tell me," I say with gritted teeth. With Joe's cheerful disposition, it has to be a lot.

"Over ten million dollars. From what the records show, Belinda opened the account after collecting her first husband's life insurance money. Aside from the insurance policy, the man came from wealth. And since he was an only child with no living relatives, Belinda was the sole beneficiary of all that cash. But you know what's even crazier?"

"I'm holding my breath," I droll out, while flipping all the details in my head.

"A week before Belinda died in the car accident, she changed her will to have her parents be the executors, with Brent as back up, until Delaina's of age," Joe says cheerfully. "She's rich, and she doesn't even know it."

"Where are Brent and Mark right now?" I demand as my anger rises to a rolling boil on Delaina's behalf.

"Last I checked, two days ago, Brent hasn't left his home in Orlando, but Mark left for Jacksonville earlier today."

"Keep a constant tab on them. And when we get close, I'll call you," I say before hanging up.

Seeing nothing but red, I pace until my temper cools,

while wrapping my head around what Joe has stumbled upon. An offshore account in her mother's name. Three businesses going under. The old man is nearly broke while the son is prospering in other endeavors. Does Delaina know about the money? I don't think so. She wouldn't have been living in that trailer otherwise.

Then, like the proverbial light bulb clicks on, everything comes together and paints a bigger picture for the reason why Brent took out the hit. It all leads to the money she didn't know about.

After taking several deep breaths to calm my racing heart, I climb back into the truck as quietly as possible. I look down at Delaina's sleeping form, softly touch her hair, and wonder how I'm going to tell her what Joe found.

"My world," I whisper to her before putting the truck into drive and continuing south.

21

D elaina

I slowly stretch the aches from my back while staring out the front window of the truck and watching Merrick play with Treg. Their backdrop, a darkening sky shadowed by purple, orange, and red with streaks of azure blue, paints a beautiful picture. One with me not in it.

Stop thinking that way, I scold myself before climbing out of the truck. "Where are we?"

"About fifty miles from Amelia City. If you need to use the bathroom." Merrick points to the building to the left.

"Umm, and where's that?"

Merrick chuckles before giving me his eyes. God, I love it when he smiles and laughs like that. But just as suddenly, all the humor is gone. "Just over the Florida border."

I nod and head to the restroom. After using the toilet, I splash some cold water on my face to wake up. Feeling slightly better, I walk out and find Treg waiting for me by the entrance. "You're my sweetheart, you know that?" I bend down and love on the animal.

Treg lavishes me with wet kisses, while his stump of a tail wags.

"Hungry?" Merrick asks as I reach the truck.

"A little." I then turn in a circle. "I didn't realize I slept so long."

"You did," he says without looking at me.

I bite my lip. "So... Then we are really doing this?"

"We are, unless you've changed your mind."

"No. I just... a little nervous," I admit sheepishly.

He diverts his eyes to the dog. "My friend has a place in Fruit Cove. He's out of the country, but he says we can stay in his house for as long as we want," Merrick explains, but he isn't looking at me.

He keeps a five-foot distance from me, and I hate the space between us. It's as though these past two weeks didn't happen and we're nothing but strangers again. Me being the mark and he, the killer.

"What aren't you saying, Merrick?" My pulse jumps with trepidation. "Tell me. I can take it." *I hope.*

"I talked to Joe while you were sleeping, and there has been a new development. I need to check it out before we proceed with the plans on confronting Brent," he says evenly, like he's being careful with his words.

"Okay. But what is it?" I insist, closing the distance. "Please, tell me."

"Right now, that's all I'm going to tell you until I confirm what Joe found. It's for your safety."

"Damn it, Merrick," I explode, inadequacy bleeding out of me. "You can't keep me in the dark. This is my life. I need to know what Joe found." Anger and tears don't mix, especially when my heart's involved, but here I am having another angry cry. In the past weeks, I've been doing that a lot.

Merrick reaches for me, but I step away. Too bad I like his dick too much to show it my knee for his high-handedness. Eventually I give in and let him swaddle me in his arms.

"Listen to me, Delaina," he whispers in my ear. "I promise you on my life that my actions are only to protect you. And once I know it's safe to tell you what he found, you'll understand why I'm holding back now."

I shake my head. "No. I won't understand."

"You're so damn stubborn, but I guess that's why I'm falling hard for you. Aunt Winnie—"

"What?" My head shoots up, meeting his gorgeous blue eyes. "You like me? More than like?"

"How can I not? You're beautiful, smart, and have one hell of a temper—one that rivals mine. Granted, this is happening so fast, but I don't care. You're everything I want in a woman," he confesses with a soft kiss to my lips.

"Well, I don't know how I feel about you," I say, totally lying to the man.

"You love me." Merrick kisses my temple. "And you trust me."

"You can't tell me I love you when I don't know for

sure if I even like you." I chuckle, and push at his chest, but he tightens his hold around me.

"That's okay. I'm patient. I can wait to hear those words."

I lean up and kiss him. "I do trust you, Merrick. Now let me go, I'm hungry," I say, understanding that he wants to keep me safe. As for telling the man how I truly feel, that will have to wait.

We get into the truck and head southeast toward Jacksonville. But the hour-long ride kick starts my brain and I re-examine the different scenarios for what Joe may have found out. Impatience getting the better of me, I start peppering Merrick with questions. However, he's steadfast in holding out.

When we pull into an exclusive subdivision, my jaw drops open at the mega mansions around us. Even in the dark, one can see this neighborhood is very wealthy, far from where I lived.

Holly Oars Court is even grander. The houses seem to grow with each structure we drive past.

"What did you say your friend does for a living?" I ask as we drive by a huge, three-story home that can easily fit a hundred of my trailers. Maybe more.

"I didn't," Merrick mumbles.

We reach the last driveway and pull up to a gate. He punches in some numbers on a key pad and the gate slides open.

"Merrick, I never..." All the words from my brain vanish like a poof of smoke when we reach the portico of the house—no, estate, we're staying in. "I don't know..."

"What are you worried about now?" He places the truck into park and turns to me. "It's only a house."

"Are you frickin' real?" I throw my arm out to the massive stucco-sided mansion before us. "This is not a house. It's practically a damn palace."

Merrick cups my neck, drawing my attention back to him. "It's a house. It's a safe place."

He climbs out, opens the back door for Treg to jump down. The dog sniffs around the pristine lawn before he lifts his leg by a large palm tree. I want to call to him to stop peeing on the tree, but that seems ridiculous on my part.

I glance back up to the monolith and a rush of air leaves my lungs. "I guess I have no choice."

"You sound like I'm torturing you by staying here," Merrick chuckles as he takes out the bags and the gun cases from the back.

"Well... maybe not torture, but I definitely am afraid of breaking anything," I admit, as I step through the double front doors. Another whoosh of air leaves my chest as I look at the grandeur of the interior.

"Come on, we'll stay in the main master suite on this floor."

My eyes widen to saucers. "There's more than one?"

Merrick laughs and shakes his head.

I follow him to the back of the *house,* past the wide-open living room space with floor to ceiling windows that look out at a river. The professional kitchen that's adjacent would make any top chef weep with joy.

Merrick heads down a long hall to the left while I take in the luxury of the space. He calls my name, but I hesitate for a second before I trail after. There's a set of open double doors I step through—and then I halt.

"I am dreaming." I take two more steps inside and slowly turn. The bedroom is rotunda shaped with a twenty-foot-high ceiling. The massive four poster king-size bed sits in the center of the room, facing a set of quad sliders that open fully. There's no obstruction to the view of the water, or the giant rectangular pool out back.

"Do you like it?" Merrick asks quietly, as though he's shy. His attitude seems odd compared to his usual gruff demeanor, but I don't question his action.

"What do I think?" I glance at him before turning my attention to the room and the view. I open my mouth to answer when his phone rings.

"Joe," he says as he stalks out of the room. I drop my backpack and follow behind. "Yeah... Okay... Good... In one hour." Merrick hangs up and turns to me.

"What's good and what's in one hour?" I ask, while keeping up with his strides.

"Be back. I'm leaving Treg here. I'll initiate the security system, so don't go past the gates. There's a heated pool out back and Treg has the lawn to roam," Merrick says before turning his back to me.

"Why can't I go with you?" I push, but Merrick grabs his small case—not his Katie, which gives me some relief he's not going out to kill anyone, but not enough to stem my anger at him for leaving me here alone. Again. "Merrick."

"Do you trust me?" Merrick moves into me, the fingers of his right hand grip my hair, and the other hand cups my face with such tenderness that I automatically lean into his touch. "Delaina, answer me. Do you trust me?"

"That's not fair," I say in a whisper as a knot of frustration grows in my chest. "I know you're going after Brent without me and that's not right. I should be there with you."

"I know, but remember, I know what I'm doing. It's best I do this alone. My way." Merrick's stubbornly set jaw contradicts how his eyes tenderly regard me.

"I do trust... you," I admit with a hitch. "But you lied. You said you'd tell me everything."

"I know. But trust me to tell you when I get back."

"Then make sure you *do* come back to me," I demand.

He kisses me with such ferocity, I nod in agreement. With his vow to come back, Merrick strides away, leaving me in a haze of want until he shuts the door, and I'm left standing alone in a house I think belongs to Merrick.

22

M errick

GLIDING ALONG DOWN I-95, the bloom of the full moon is my companion. Hugging my body against the Ducati Streetfighter V4, my blood is humming with excitement. This is my first time riding this machine, and what a ride it is. Between the speed this vehicle can reach and the thrum of the engine between my legs, the motorcycle was worth every penny.

If there are any cops along the way, the speed of this bike will blow them away.

It's past midnight and I have over an hour's ride to Windemere. Given the sufficient lighting from the moon, I keep the headlight off, wanting the least amount of attention on me.

Coming in like a thief is my goal. I want to grab Brent Miller's full attention before he alerts any cops or security from his neighborhood.

Easing up on the throttle, I merge onto I-4 and then gun it. Soon after, I pull onto Butler Street and hide my bike in a copse of dense wisteria that segues to the beach four houses away from Brent's.

Scanning the area, there's no activity on the street or at the surrounding houses. But that's what I'd expect for the middle of the night on a Tuesday.

Quickly looking over the schematics Joe texted me of Brent Miller's house, the best point of entry is clear.

Avoiding the lights set around the house, I head to the small box on the side of the house and disable the alarm system. Then I head to the back of the house, where the landscape slopes down.

I climb up a trellis that's filled with purple flowers at the back left corner of the house. The elaborate wooden structure arches under the second-floor kitchen.

The layout of the home is weird to me, but it works to my advantage as I take my KA-BAR out again and use the knife to pry open the window over the large stainless steel farmhouse sink.

Once both feet are firm on the floor, I find the staircase to the basement and quietly descend the stairs, to where the breaker box is located. With a single switch, the entire house is in the dark. Then I head up to the main master bedroom on the other end of the seven thousand square foot house.

Heading down the hallway, I immediately take in the sparse grandeur of the space. There isn't much on the walls; it's like all of the art has been removed. Come to think about it, there isn't much furniture either.

When I reach the bedroom door, a sudden need to get the fuck out of there gnarls up in my gut. This house looks empty. Like Brent doesn't live here anymore. If that's the case...

Fuck.

I spin toward the main part of the house, to the back where I entered. Just past what looks like a study, I hear something. A door creaking open. I stop, unsheathe my knife and step back into an empty den, leaving the door ajar.

Scanning the walls of empty bookshelves and the clunky desk in the middle of the room, my assessment has to be right. Brent doesn't live here—or hasn't for some time. Then why did Joe tell me Brent still does? I'll deal with him later.

Another creak—this time in the hallway, and I let out a quiet breath and ready myself. I can see two shadowy figures through the crack of the door. They silently stalk toward the room I'm in. Dressed in black like myself, one guy stops right at the door and nods to his partner to check the other room. I ready myself knowing this will be a kill-or-be-killed situation.

With a heavy boot, the first guy kicks the door fully open, slamming it against the wall. Knowing the asshole's move, I side-step out of the crush and crouch. The moment the bastard rushes inside, I launch—knife out—blade right to the back of his knee. I slice deep, cutting into the tendon.

His silencer goes off as I lash out again, leaving a bloody trail in my wake. The guy drops, still shooting at everything but me.

Then the second asshole jumps into the fray, a flashlight now on his shoulder. I don't think twice as I dive at the bulk of the guy and jam my knife into his throat. A gurgling sound echoes off the walls before the Reaper takes him.

With one guy dead and the other whimpering as he tries to scramble out of the room, this is my one chance to find out who is behind this and where the fuck Brent is.

After I kick the gun out of the man's hand, I point the knife to his throat. "Who sent you?"

He shoots me a glare. With a foot to that injured leg, I press hard, which has him screaming in pain.

"I'll ask you again. Who sent you?"

"I don't know." Blood seeps out of the asshole's mouth.

I put more pressure on the leg. "Lie."

"I swear," he grits out another cry of pain. "My partner got a text on where to go and what time—that's it." His head slumps onto the floor. "You killed him," he whispers.

I ignore his comment. "Where's Brent Miller?"

"I don't know. The text said the house would be empty and to kill the intruder. That's all."

I pick up the gun, look at it for a second, aim it at the man's head and shoot. Then I search his partner's pockets for the cell phone. After I find it, I walk out of the house, not bothering with the bodies.

With each step to my bike, I become more certain that I was set up by the only person who knew where I was going. The one person who thought he'd fooled me. "I'm coming for you, Joe."

23

D elaina

A GROWL from Treg wakes me instantly as a chill trickles down my spine. He wouldn't growl if it was Merrick. That being the case, I slowly climb out of bed, slide on my slippers, and carefully walk to the closed bedroom door.

With Treg's hackles up, I press my ear to the wall, close my eyes and listen. Nothing but the sounds of a quiet house—then I hear it. Something. Footsteps.

I take a single step back as the door crashes open, knocking me down in the process. Treg launches himself at whoever storms inside the room.

Three gunshots go off. I scream, as Treg drops with a yelp.

Stumbling backward, everything's hazy for a second

before I identify the person that crashed into the room. Mark.

"Bastard!" I launch myself at my stepbrother, knocking the gun out of his hand before he shoots Treg again. Mark might be bigger and stronger than me, but I get in a punch to his face. Though my satisfaction is short-lived. He back-hands me, easily knocking me off balance.

I drop—hitting the back of my head on the floor. Pain reverberates through my skull, turning my vision blurry.

"Bitch," he hisses before grabbing me by the hair and yanking me up to stand. With an open palm, he slaps me and blood floods my mouth. "This time, you won't get away from me. You'll mind me, Delaina. Or I'll beat submission into you."

"I will never..." My words catch in my throat at the sight of Treg not moving.

Treg. I'm sorry, Merrick.

"You will never what?" The rage in Mark's hazel eyes sends a wave of fear throughout my body. "You're forgetting something, love. You are mine and nothing's going to change that."

I've been afraid of my stepbrother before, but not like this. He's psychotic, and I'm truly terrified for my life, so scared I can't speak.

"Yeah, figured that."

Without another word, he drags me out of the room, out the front door of the house, and into a waiting black Navigator that's idling in the driveway, like kidnapping is an every night occurrence. I just hope Merrick gets home in time to save Treg.

I should have told Merrick how I feel about him back while we were in Vermont. And now, deep in my heart, I know I'll never get the chance to tell Merrick I love him.

Before Mark slams the back door, he idly stares at me like he's waiting for me to say something. But I stay mute, since he's more terrifying than ever and I can't decipher what he wants.

However, I don't have to wonder for long, because Mark cocks back his arm and that's the last thing I see before blackness overcomes me.

24

M errick

The eerie silence drags along my spine like a honed knife as I quietly step inside through the side door of my house.

Something's wrong. I can feel it in the air. I tap the light on in the laundry room, but I remain in the dark.

Fucking Christ. If Joe got to Delaina, the devil is the least of his worries.

I pull out my 9 mm while pausing in the kitchen. With a calm breath, I listen for any sounds. A far-off whine catches my ears and causes my insides to shred. It's Treg, and he's hurt.

I cautiously race to the bedroom I left Delaina in. With the gun aimed and ready by the broken door, my heart drops at the sight before me. Treg lies on his side, with a bloom of red near his rear flank. The damn dog's wagging his tail when he sees me.

Reflexively, I look around the space, seeing the disaster of the room. There's only one possible conclusion, Delaina is gone and not by her own choice.

By whose, I'll soon find out. But Treg comes first.

Reaching my dog in four long strides, I quickly assess how badly he's hurt. Treg being alert gives me some hope he's not dying.

I call the vet that's on my speed dial while picking Treg up and carrying him to the truck.

Once I get Treg into the vet's hands, and hear that he'll live, I head back to the house. In my surveillance room, I examine different camera footages from around the house and grounds. Sure enough, there was a blacked-out SUV idling by the gate.

The driver's window slides down, exposing the bastard's face. Mark Miller.

He punches in the code and the gate opens. Mark Miller gets out of the vehicle. Like he owns this fucking property, he waltzes into my house and heads straight to the master bedroom.

How did he know to come here?

That prick didn't have any qualms about hitting Delaina again, before dragging her out of the house. As each second clicks past on the monitor, the gnawing in my gut tells me who's working with Mark. "Fucking Joe."

It's the only plausible conclusion I can come up with. This entire time, that motherfucker has been playing me. But this game isn't over.

Before I left, I was smart enough to place a tiny tracker in Delaina's hair, in case of something—I don't know—maybe she had the right idea to follow me. The device mimics a small sparkly jewel a woman would use in her hair. But this little gadget will help me find her. And Mark.

But I have one more task to do before I go after Delaina. I'm sending a message to Joe from a phone I have saved for a special occasion. The cell has a virus embedded in it. I got the phone and virus off of a black hat hacker a few years back as payment for a job. She guaranteed me no other hacker can detect the virus in his system until it launches. And since Joe's wired from cell to screen, he won't know what's hit him until it's too late.

With a wide smile on my face, I grab the phone from my safe, and text three words to Joe.

You're next, Motherfucker. Then I hit send.

I don't wait to see a response. With truck keys in hand, I take off in the direction Delaina's tracker is blinking. Mark's heading down the coastal highway A1A.

"Where are you going, asshole?" I growl to myself.

Since he has a good two hours on me, I know time is of the essence to reach Delaina before Mark does something to her. Between keeping an eye on the road and on Delaina's trace on my phone, I put the pedal down to the floor and center my rage on what I'm going to do to Mark Miller.

25

D elaina

PAIN RADIATES from my left eye and cheek as I slowly wake and look around me. My arms and legs are tied to the bedposts. And I'm naked. Frantically I look around and see the room is filled with lit candles as though it's set up as a romantic night for a couple.

Horror courses through every inch of my body as I desperately yank at the ropes biting into my wrists and ankles.

This isn't happening. Please, tell me this isn't happening.

"I'm sorry I had to hit you," Mark says from in the shadows. He's in a chair at the end of the bed. "You know I find your face so beautiful, but you gave me no choice."

Icy dread races up my spine, and it has everything to do with this monster before me.

My body begins to shake profusely. "Why am I tied up, Mark? Let me go, please." I struggle to calm my fear of him, but I can't stop trembling.

"I don't want you to leave me again. You got to understand, Delaina. You're mine," he states matter-of-factly, like we're a couple.

"I was never yours," I bite out and yank at the ropes again. "You're delusional."

A growl tears from Mark's mouth and he launches onto the bed, bringing his maniacal face just inches from mine. "You've been mine since you were sixteen years old. You gave me your virginity. Don't you remember?" Spit lands on my cheeks, and I have to turn my face away.

I close my eyes as panic grips me and every bit of air in my lungs leaves. No matter how much I want to deny his words, I clamp my mouth shut and remain still as he rages against me.

"When I found out that you were fucking that guy— that killer, I had to do something."

My eyes snap to his, and the question automatically bursts out of me with no restraints. "What are you talking about?"

"You see, Delaina. I've known where you were the entire time. What you've been doing with that fucker. I've been biding my time until I got a chance to kill that bastard for touching you. I would have done it myself, but Joe says it's better this way," Mark rambles on.

"Joe?" Merrick's Joe? The same Joe who's been helping

Merrick and me? This whole time he's been helping Mark? "Why?"

Mark's features soften and he smiles as his hand begins to caress my left breast like it's a pet. He's even more disturbed than before. "Because I told you, that filthy killer touched what's mine."

"Why did you hire killers to murder me?" My shaky voice sounds wrong to my own ears.

"You got it wrong, baby. You see, I hired them to scare you. I wanted you to run to me for help. That greedy asshole thinks he's turned the tables on me, but he's wrong. I saw an opportunity and took it. What *he* doesn't understand is that I have all the cards."

"All the cards?" I ask with revulsion.

"I got you and the money, honey." He runs a hand from my leg to my breast and squeezes hard.

I grimace at his touch, but it won't stop me from asking how he got Joe to work with him.

"I don't understand how you turned Joe against Merrick."

"Don't say that fucker's name in my presence." The pain he delivers to my nipple has me biting back a cry. I won't give him the satisfaction. He pulls back and studies me. "If you want to really know, I'll tell you."

I expect him to say the million dollars he has on killing me, but I'm wrong.

"Even more money than the million I stole from my father," Mark says, as he leans in and sniffs my hair. "I always loved the way you smell."

"From where?" I ask, hoping he still has some sense to tell me.

But Mark loses his smile, pinches my nipple hard again and I clamp my teeth down on my lip.

"Kiss me." He leans in and without waiting for my permission or denial, he plants a kiss on my lips. He tries shoving his tongue in my mouth, but I refuse to open for him and get another sharp bite of pain on my sore nipple.

This time I cry out and Mark dives in open mouthed like a greedy bottom feeder would do. I bite his tongue, and he immediately yanks away and backhands my face. Stars burst across my vision, and I see two of him. Though, I'd take his hand instead of having his mouth on me again. Mark swipes his mouth with the back of his hand and comes away with blood.

"You fucking bitch. You could have bit off my tongue." He squares back onto his knees, which are wedged between my spread legs. I know his torture isn't over, because of the blatant craziness shining in his bloodshot eyes.

"Good." I spit at him, not caring anymore if he hurts me again. As for Joe, once Merrick finds out he's involved, the guy is going to die. I know it as well as I know I'm breathing.

"Good?" He huffs out a laugh as he climbs off the bed. "You'll change your tune once I'm done with you."

Tendrils of dread snake along my naked flesh as he chuckles and begins to take off his clothes. "What are you doing?"

"Since playing nice isn't going to work, I'm going to do

bad things to you until you give in to me. And you're going to want it, Delaina. Just like I loved you at sixteen. But this time, I won't be gentle. This time, I'm going to fuck you until you bleed again—until you accept my love."

A cry of terror leaves my lips as he drops his shirt and starts undoing his pants. Just as he slips his leather belt from his waist, I close my eyes and try to reach in deep and find my happy place. The one person who makes me feel safe and cherished. "Merrick," I whisper.

"He won't be saving you, sweetheart. Your precious Merrick is dead."

"No," I utter in disbelief as tears stream out the corners of my eyes. I open them and peer at the monster standing at the foot of the bed. "Merrick's the best at what he does. He's not dead." I shake my head in denial.

"Yes, he is," Mark chortles as though I'm the fool. "There's no one but me for you to love."

"I will never love you, Mark. Never." My oath whips out of me, as angry as the rage emanating from my stepbrother's eyes.

He loops his belt and gives it a sharp whack against his open palm, and the sound ricochets off the walls. "You'll change your mind, once I'm done with you. Now, sweetheart, punishment first before I give you the good fucking you need."

"No, please," I whisper, slamming my eyes shut and bracing for the pain.

A soft thud and a gurgle has me opening my eyes. The candles around us are flickering from the now open patio door.

Nausea roils in my stomach as I slowly look at Mark. He's standing there still as a statue, eyes wide with utter disbelief. His hands are at his neck and his mouth is gaping open like a largemouth bass. My eyes travel to his clutching hands, and I finally see it. Blood dripping down his chest.

"You touched what's mine," Merrick growls before he comes out of the shadow and shoves Mark. My stepbrother stumbles forward, his eyes roll back into his skull, and he falls dead to the floor.

26

M errick

"Merrick," Delaina cries out as she yanks on the ropes that bind her arms.

Seeing her bruised, naked, and bound has been a torture. But I needed Mark to answer the question about Joe. And I was right. This betrayal is over fucking money.

I cut the ropes around her wrists and ankles and then scoop her up into my arms, cradling her to me, because she's the most precious thing I have in my life, next to Treg.

"He said you were dead." She presses hard to the crook of my neck.

"He's wrong," I say as I squeeze her tighter and kiss her forehead.

"I'm glad," she utters, tipping her head back and showing her beautiful watery smile. Tears keep leaking from her eyes, but they are happy ones. "What about Joe?"

"He's not going anywhere. You come first." I grab a blanket from the bed and wrap Delaina in it. Then I carry her out of the house and gently put her in the passenger seat of my truck. "Be right back." I close the door and turn back to the house.

"Where are you going?" Her panic voice reaches me.

I turn back around and smile. "I have to clean up, but it won't take long. Promise."

I guess my oath is enough because Delaina's body visibly relaxes against the seat, and she nods at me.

Without hesitation, I head back into the house, clean anything I touched and remove any remnants of Delaina being present in the home. After I've deleted all images from the asshole's cheap security surveillance system, I skim the inner part of the house, the bedroom where the lit candles are and Mark's body with lighter fluid. I pull out a match, ignite the flame and drop it. That should do the trick.

Since I deactivated the alarm on the house, it's going to take some time before someone sees the house on fire. By the time the fire department arrives, every bit of Mark Miller's body will be charred and sent to hell.

With one final glance around, I leave and drive off back to my house.

As we head up A1A, I make a call to one of my go-to's to get rid of the truck, since it most definitely has been seen in the area.

We make the quick trade in Melbourne, one truck for

another. Different color, different model, and definitely newer year. Clean plates and cleaner interior.

I breathe better knowing Delaina is finally safe and out of harm's way. But I can't be lax when I don't trust Mable's word about retribution. We'll have to see.

And I still have Brent to find and Joe to destroy. So I make one more call. Connecting my cell phone to the truck's Bluetooth, I hit the number I've only used once before.

"Sabrina," I say, my eyes meeting Delaina's as I put my finger to my lips. She nods in understanding, and I return my attention to the road.

"Merrick, I was wondering when I would be hearing from you. I heard through the grapevine you've been having some trouble," the female says with a hint of humor to her tone.

"You can say that," I admit, knowing there's no point in hiding the truth from Sabrina. Next to Joe, she's one of the best hackers out there. "I need your help."

"I figured that, since you called me." She chuckles and then clears her throat. "What do I get in return for helping you?"

"I had a feeling you'd ask that. What do you want?"

"Two things," she says briskly.

"And they are?"

"I want to take down Joe and take over his job," she states with ferocity.

"Joe is my problem, and I might be retiring. Unless..."

"Unless what?" she asks, sounding like an eager puppy wanting play time.

"I need you to track down one Brent Miller—"

"Done," she quickly cuts in.

"Find Joe. I'll deal with him. And..."

"Yes?" she says with a chuckle.

"Since you're temporarily working for me, book two round trip plane tickets to Raleigh and a week's stay in a nice hotel, one month from now."

"That's it?" Sabrina asks with a snit.

"Do you want more?" I ask, finally looking over at Delaina. Her head's angled back against the headrest. Warmth fills my chest knowing she trusts me enough to relax.

"Whatever," Sabrina says with a snap in her tone. "Will have both details to you soon." She hangs up.

Gently, I hold Delaina's small hand as I drive us back to Fruit Cove. The plans are to retrieve Treg the following day from the vet, then pack up and go to the only place that feels like home to me.

Epilogue

D elaina

IT'S BEEN ALMOST a month since we arrived back at
Merrick's Vermont homestead, and we're all faring well.
Treg's doing fine. The gunshot wound damaged his hind
leg, but the vet did a fantastic job removing the bullet with
little issue. Now, he's lying next to me on the sofa, in front
of the fireplace, sleeping like he's the king of the castle.

My period showed up yesterday, confirming I'm not
pregnant, which I knew a week ago when I took a preg-
nancy test. Would I love to have babies with Merrick?
Someday, when my life is normal and I know we are truly
safe.

I wish my thoughts were as easy as the dog's demeanor,
though. I still worry about any retaliation or backlash from
this Mable woman. Merrick promises that I'm safe and not

to worry about the hitwoman. But I can't help it. He did kill three of her sons to save my life.

I shudder at the memories of what happened in Florida and my first time in Vermont. If it weren't for Merrick, I'd be dead. It's funny to think that it took a hitman to protect me. And it's even more fantastical that I fell in love with him through all the insanity. Although, I still haven't told him how I feel.

As for my stepfather, Sabrina found out where Brent was. He'd been hiding in a condo down in Marco Island. When the police got to him, he confessed he was hiding from his crazed son.

The money Brent's talking about is from a Raleigh account that belongs to me, of which I had no clue. When my grandparents passed away, I was still a minor, so Brent became my guardian. He was able to access the cash as his personal ATM. When I turned eighteen, all rights shifted to me, and he had no access. So he forged my signature to get back into the account.

Mark found out what Brent was doing and threatened him for access to the cash. Since his father wasn't able to grant Mark's demands, Brent went into hiding, fearing his son would kill him. That's where Merrick ended the explanation.

Where does Joe fit into all this? I still don't know. Whenever I ask Merrick about his former handler, he ignores me. Okay, not really *ignores* me. My gorgeous hitman kisses me thoroughly to shut me up and loves on me in every glorious possible way.

Hmmm. My girlie parts are thrumming just thinking

about Merrick's talented, well-hung cock.

"What's going on in that head of yours?" Merrick stands in front of me, crowding into my space. I'm face to face with his groin.

"Wouldn't you like to know?" I tip my head back and look into his blue depths and smirk. "Merrick—"

"Got a call from Sabrina. She knows where Joe's hiding," he says evenly as he pulls me to my feet. The coldness in his eyes when he mentions Joe's name sets off a chill throughout the warm room.

"Where is he?" I ask with trepidation.

Merrick caresses my face as a small smile forms across his lips, which unnerves me. "Get your bags packed. We're leaving tomorrow for Raleigh."

"I hate it when you don't answer my question." The lustful thoughts that were coursing through me suddenly shift to pure elation at the mention of the impending trip.

Excitement swirls in the pit of my stomach. I'm going to find out how much money I have left in the account my mother had set up. Then a somber thought hits me. Maybe the account is wrong and there's hardly any money left to start a new life. What if Brent used it all? I guess that old adage is correct, *You can't miss what you never had.*

But I do have. Thanks to my parents.

I release a breath and slump against Merrick. My eyes drop to the floor, while pondering what the next step in my life will be.

Merrick's hands skim through my hair, gently tipping my head back until our eyes meet. "You mean more to me than anything, Delaina. No amount of money will ever change the way I feel for you. You will always be safe with me. I will protect you with my life. Remember that. And from this point on, whatever it may be, *we'll* do it together." His solemn oath quickly soothes the rawness of my emotions.

"I don't know why I worry about the money," I say, wrapping my arms around him.

Merrick pulls a piece of paper out of his back pocket and hands it to me. "Then let me put you at ease."

I scan what looks like a bank document. When I get to the bottom figure, my eyes go wide and I stammer out, "There's... over f-five... million dollars."

"Yes," Merrick answers softly, like he's afraid to talk any louder or he'd spook me. But he did anyway.

My eyes lift to meet his with trepidation. "This can't be. Brent had full access to the account when I turned eighteen. I thought there would be nothing left. I can't believe that amount of money is mine."

"It's yours. All of it," Merrick says evenly as he points to the top of the page, where my name is.

"You mean ours," I correct, leaning up and kissing him. "We are in this together."

Merrick's arms tighten. "Together."

A burst of emotion has me tearing up, so trying to jail in the vow is useless. "I love you, Merrick."

Merrick scoops me up, carries me to the bedroom and gently puts me on the bed.

"Look at me," he demands, and I meet his eyes. "I love you, too." Then my hitman shows me just how much he loves me.

Epilogue II
Two Weeks Later

Merrick

It won't be hard entering the condo where Joe's hiding himself away from me. It's actually laughable that he thinks he can outrun me, especially when his betrayal runs just as deep as my anger.

We had five long years of successful partnering. But I guess money is more important than loyalty between us. I'll rectify that soon.

With Sabrina's detailed report, Joe's place is on the twelfth floor of this downtown Chicago high-rise. Entering the building was easy. With a fake nose, glasses, and a full beard, I walk in as though I belong here.

I hand the security guard my false identification and explain why I'm there and give the name of the building manager, who happens to be waiting on the thirteenth floor to show me an empty condo I'm supposedly looking to rent. Since my fake name is on the list, I waltz past the security desk and straight to the elevator.

Right after I tap the up arrow, I send the manager a quick text that I'm twenty minutes away. Then I step inside, press thirteen and still my movements. Sabrina hacked into the security system already, and put it on a repeat loop in the elevator camera. Once I get the go-ahead, I hit floor twelve.

Again, Sabrina fixed the security camera on that floor. The door slides open, and I have less than five to claim my revenge.

Drawing close to Joe's door, in my earpiece I hear Sabrina laughing her ass off. "What's so fucking funny?" I whisper.

"He's...," laugh. "...at it," snort. "...again."

What the hell? "Explain," I grunt out as I quickly look around me to make sure none of Joe's neighbors are in the hallway.

"Remember that virus I gave you as payment a few years back?"

"Open the door," I utter as I glance over my shoulder to the empty hallway. "What about it? I used it on Joe."

"I know," she snorts. "He's having trouble with it now."

There's a click from the electronic lock as it disengages. I quietly push open the door and enter the condo. With a gentle push, the door silently closes without the alarms going off.

Jesus. I'm standing in the entryway, staring at what's supposed to be an open concept living and kitchen area, but several things are missing. Furniture.

As I step around the corner, I hear Joe's voice. He's loud and swearing his ass off.

If it weren't for Joe handing me the job that marked Delaina, I wouldn't be standing here now questioning my ex-handler on why he betrayed me.

I silently thank him for sending me to Delaina, but I'm still going to put a bullet through his brain. A betrayal is a betrayal. And greed does corrupt, except where Delaina is concerned. It was all about survival for her.

I have to inwardly laugh, remembering when we were in Raleigh and Delaina announced to me that she was going to take care of me with her money. I put her straight while we were in our hotel room bed, me inside her, and told her the truth about the money I've saved. I swear she nearly had a heart attack when I told how much.

Now, we're blissfully happy... except for one last act to tie up the final loose end.

"I hear him," I whisper to Sabrina.

"Don't kill him yet," she says with another chortle of laughter. "See what he's pissed about first before you end him."

That's one thing I like about Sabrina, she doesn't mince words.

"Will do."

I creep down the hall, toward the last room. The door is partially open, it's dark—aside from the light emanating from the several monitors hung on the wall.

Then I see it.

"What am I looking at?" I ask her, for a second

thinking I'm watching a kid show until I see dicks and pussies exposed from furry costumes.

"Furry porn!" she screeches in my ear. "Every time he uses a certain code, my virus kicks up and every screen will pop up to these sites," she says with another round of laughter.

I want to also laugh, but the last thing I need is for Joe to grab for his weapon. I click off my headset, cutting off Sabrina's laughter and ready my 9 mm, aiming it at my ex-handler's head. With a soft whistle, Joe swivels his head to me like it's a slow-motion action shot.

Sure enough, he has a gun—a Zoraki 9, in his clutches. "I knew you'd show up," Joe says shakily, as he darts his attention between me and the door.

"There's no escape, Joe." I focus my aim at his forehead.

He belligerently points the gun at me like he has a chance of getting out of this alive. But he's wrong. All Joe's going to do is piss his pants.

I'll take a picture of that for Sabrina.

"Sure, there is. Especially now since I knew you were coming after me." Joe's whining pulls me from my musing.

"The operative word is *were*." I drop my silencer enough and squeeze the trigger, the bullet aimed for his hand.

A howl of pain leaves Joe's lips. He drops the gun and a trigger finger along with it.

"You fucking shot my right hand. I will never be able to use it," he shouts.

I ignore his screams and ask a question of my own. "Why did you betray me? Are you that fucking greedy?"

"Every penny counts, asshole," he grits out in agony. "Every, penny."

"So does betrayal." Too disgusted to listen to more of his crying, I squeeze the trigger and put a bullet between his eyes. I click my ear bud back on. "It's done," I say to Sabrina.

"Alrighty, boss man. Money is wired to the account... minus my sign-on bonus," she says with a chuckle. "Once you're gone, I'll wipe clean any evidence and video footage that has you in it."

"Thanks." With one last look at Joe's lifeless body, I leave as quietly as I came, my mind on home, where my woman and dog are waiting for me.

CJ's Note to the Readers

Dear Reader,

I want to thank you so much for getting Protecting Delaina. I truly enjoyed writing these two characters and the journey they took me on in finding their happily ever after.

Even though, this book is a single title, you will be seeing Merrick again in an upcoming series I'm currently working on. Granted, the story is still raw, but here's a sneak peek of a couple chapters in the first book of this MMF dark romantic thriller series.

And please, help me out and leave a review on all the viable platforms. I'd truly appreciate it.

Want more details of the upcoming books, events and signings I'll be at? Join me in my group, subscribe to my newsletter, and follow! https://linktr.ee/cjwarrant

Smooches,

CJ

About CJ Warrant

Award-Winning Author CJ Warrant was born an overseas Army brat, in a Korean Italian household, but settled in the states at five. She also has an alter ego, CJ Barlowe, who writes MM romance.

CJ had a career in the beauty industry, a wonderful supportive hubby, three grown kids and new cat mom. When she's not writing, she hangs with her family, bake, or just chill with a book.

To get to know me more, please follow, like and subscribe:

https://linktr.ee/cjwarrant

Also by CJ Warrant

<u>Contemporary Romance</u>

Sweet Reunion

Sweet Redemption

Landry Brothers Bundle Pack

<u>Saints vs Sinners Series</u>

Deacon – Book 1

<u>Dark Supernatural Thriller</u>

Forgetting Jane

Dance of the Mourning Cloak

<u>Dark Erotic Thrillers</u>

Mirror Image

<u>A Chance At Love Novella MM Romance Series</u>

Four Days

One Kiss

Five Seasons of Love

Two Of Hearts

Three Times Lucky

<u>Boba Book Babes Mysteries</u>

Pandemonium In Peoria

Coming Soon- Silenced in San Antonio

We All Fall Down Series

A Dark MMF Romantic Suspense

Regina's Diary
May 2, 2007

Dear Diary,

It was the worst Wednesday ever. It was Terrible with the capital T. It started with a note my best friend, Maya passed me in math class.

Who do you like more? Who would you kiss? Krew Gatlin or Decker Moss?

They are the two most popular seventh graders in Granger Middle school, Diary. All the girls—including us fifth graders like them.

They were harmless questions Maya asked me, so I wrote back, I like them both. But I never answered the kissing question, Diary, because I really didn't know. I never kissed a boy, ever!

I didn't think that note would cause me so much trouble.

But when I passed the note back to Maya, my teacher—the jerk—Mr. Trince, grabbed it out of my hand and started reading it out loud in front of the class. Do you believe that, Diary?!

I was so embarrassed. I covered my face with both hands and wanted to cry. But I didn't.

Thank goodness, Krew and Decker wasn't in that class or in my grade, but I was afraid they would hear about it anyway.

And I was right. The kids in my class talked, and Krew and Decker found out. At lunch hour, they scowled at me from the across the lunch room. Right then, I knew they hated my guts.

Maya felt bad for sending me the note, but it was a too late.

I'm never ever going to school ever again.

Love,
Regi

Prologue

R egina

Every frantic, stumbling step I took through the dark woods was one step further from *him*. I couldn't tell if the coppery taste of blood in my mouth was mine, or from the asshole who'd ripped away my innocence—my soul, with each forceful thrust as his body invaded mine.

With each hard swallow, the pain grew, like razor blade clawing down the back of my throat. A vivid memory slammed into my head at how he'd clamped his hard, filthy hand around my neck, and squeezed until his blunt fingernails dug into my skin. Or how he'd punched me in the face a couple of times to stop me from screaming.

I swiped my swollen tongue along my split lower lip, and a sharp sting made me wince.

As I raced through the trees toward the open clearing, a monster size desperation filled my gut, warning me to keep looking back over my shoulder. I prayed the bastard wasn't following me.

Finally, I came to the edge of the woods and found it to be a corn field. I choked out a silent relieved sob as fat tears blurred my vision.

I hurried on, oblivious to the row of stubs left over from the fall harvest. The sharp protruding husks were like dull knives cutting into the tender sole of my left foot, but not the other. For some miraculous reason, my favorite flip flop was still on my right foot, even after I escaped.

The sting gave me some temporary relief from the throbbing pain between my legs.

Keep moving, I told myself as my heart rate ratcheted up and the pounding in my ears got louder. No matter what, I had to run faster, had to find a hiding place before *he* saw me out in the open. Because if he caught up with me, I knew I'd be dead for what I had done to him.

He'd raped me, but I'd fought back. And I was certain the gouges I'd made with my nails would scar his face.

The icy wind and the sliver of waning moon in the dark sky added to the horror and dread flooding my veins. I didn't want to think about that—think about *him*, or what he could do—not when I had already endured hell.

Noise from behind had me dropping to the ground and stiffening like a statue. My heart thundered furiously against my ribcage, the hammering echoing in my ears intensified, and stars burst across my vision. I was going to pass out, but I refused to close my bruised eyes.

I swept a cautious look along the field and found loose

corn leaves rustling along the uneven ground. Then I saw it. In the distance were twin lights. *Headlights.*

Hope caused the panic that was piercing my chest spiked up. It was a road. And that meant my phone could finally work and I could call for help.

I heaved myself back onto my feet and ran as swiftly as I could in the direction of the road, still keeping a feverish eye back toward the woods.

With the struggle to breath, the pain intensified with each hard step, and the hatred in my heart swarming like killer bees, my anxiety was on a knife's edge. But I kept on running.

Every few steps, I glanced down at the cell phone clutched in my hand. There were no bars. Yet. Even with dread creeping back in, I had no other choice but to keep moving. I wouldn't die here—not here—not where he would find me.

Clinging to a thin thread of hope, I finally reached the trench by the road. Clutching my torn shirt, I decided to drop into it. But I tripped and tumbled down, face-first and then to my side. Pain wracked my entire body. I waited for the dizziness to clear before checking for bars on my phone.

I was so focused on running and finding a safe hiding place, I hadn't realized that I was bleeding. My hand came away from between my legs wet and red. A soft cry tore through me as I tried to block out what had been done to me. I fixated on the cracked screen of the cell phone, still gripped in my hand.

I straightened the best I could, and prayed I got reception.

"Two bars," I uttered in relief, and then quickly pressed my thumb down on the button, and shakily uttered, "Siri, call Maya's cell..."

Please, Siri answer. I repeated the mantra in my head, while my heavy breaths sawed in and out of my sore lungs.

Ten full seconds into the silence... and, "Calling Maya's cell," Siri robotically said.

I held my breath while the call connected, clinging to the chance that the Maya would pick up right away.

"Girl, do you know what time—"

I wept louder at the sound of her voice. "Maya... I need—"

A shout of rage echoed through the night air, and I froze, the cell pressed to my wet cheek. I didn't know in what direction the scream came from, but I immediately plastered myself to the cold, damp ground. Fear spiked like an erupting volcano and I began to shake uncontrollably as the thought of being raped again shredded through my soul.

I forgot in that moment that Maya was on the phone. I was so lost to the frightening despair and pain that I didn't hear my best friend yelling my name.

"Regi! What's going on?" Her voice had ultimately cut into my living nightmare. "Where are you?"

"I... need, help," I whispered hoarsely, all my energy was slowly seeping out from me.

"Let me call your par—"

"No. Please, don't call them. Just come and get me," I pleaded, as a torrent of tears blurred my vision once again.

"Hold on," she said. "Don't hang up. I'm seeing if I can locate you... Jesus! How did you get all the way out to Dixon County Woods?"

I didn't even know where that was. "Hurry," I frantically uttered as I pulled the phone away and listened harder for more sounds, then whispered, "Before he finds me."

"Who—who is after you?"

"Please," I cried, not able to say his name out loud.

"Okay... Hang tight, girl. It's going to be a bit."

"O-k—." Then the phone went dead. The battery died.

No! I inwardly screamed. I tried shaking the phone, but there was no reception, no light came from the screen. It was dead. And so was I. Maya was never going to find me.

I curled myself into a ball, my dead cell phone to my chest, and shut down.

My beautiful morning had been ripped into a million fractured shards the second Decker, Krew, and I climbed into his brother's car. And deep down in my soul, I knew, the moment I was separated from my guys, that my life would never be the same again. Ever.

Plagued by utter fear and the cold slithering into my body, I wasn't sure how long I laid in that trench, but it had to be quite some time because I was numb down to the bone.

Hallucinations rattled my thoughts, and when a

familiar voice called my name, I thought *This is it. I'm dying.*

Or so close to it. as I laid in the cold, dark dank ditch. I even bet myself that they wouldn't find my body until I was well decomposed.

But then I heard my best friend's voice again, which startled me out of my dismal frame of mind.

"Maya," I called out in a croaked whisper. Whatever energy was left in my body, I launched my arm upward as a bright light was cast over me. It might as well have been the sun shining down on me, because I had a reason to smile.

"Jesus fucking Christ, Regi—Who—Oh my God..."

Using nothing but pure grit, I dragged my tired and battered body up from the ground and hugged my best friend.

Chapter One
Current Day

Regi

"I don't know how you talk me into these things, Maya. Are you sure this is all legal?"

"Stop worrying. Jess said it's all good," my best friend replied without looking at me. Her attention was solely on searching the crowd for Jess, her man of the month.

"I don't care what Jess said, I want to leave. This isn't my type of place to hang out." I gripped Maya's arm and tried tugging her back toward the entryway. This seedy abandoned warehouse, in a less-than-reputable area of Chicago, gave me the heebie-jeebies.

"You're not leaving, Regi. God, girl. It's Saturday night, and you never go out. We're here now. So, let's have some fun." Maya yanked out of my hold, clasped my hand, and pulled me—and my simple black dress, through a crowd of well-dressed people.

Most of the men were in expensive suits, but the women—including Maya—were glitzed up, like they were in an exclusive nightclub and were here to dance the night away. This place was like no night club I'd ever been to.

"Fun?" I hissed in her ear. "Watching two people beating the crap out of each other isn't fun, Maya."

"Then close your eyes," she hissed, before casting a glance over her shoulder at me and smiling, all the angry bravado gone. "Stop being a bore, Regi. Besides, maybe you'll meet somebody here. Get laid—anything to get that old lady stick out of your ass."

"I don't have a stick up my ass," I huffed out. And what the heck does she mean by old lady? But I didn't ask.

Maya whirled around. "Yes, you do. Ever since you took over for Diana, all you do is work and sleep. I'm surprised you even had time to put on makeup tonight."

I snorted. Maya was ridiculous. "At least..." I bit my lower lip from saying anything hurtful.

"What? Say it." She got in my face.

"Nothing." I backed down. There was no point in arguing with her. My best friend had been there for me in the most trying times of my life, and throwing trash back in her face wasn't nice. It wasn't me.

"Girl, it's been ages since you let down your hair—or what hair you have left on your head, and had some fun. Do it for me. Please. We don't have to stay long. I promise." Damn it, I hated when she gave me the puppy dog eyes.

"Fine," I dragged out.

"Great," she chirped, then circled her fingers around

my wrist and dragged me further down a desolate corridor, deeper into the bowels of the building.

With crumbling cement walls, holes in the floors and ceiling, and rebars protruding out here and there, I wouldn't be surprised if someone who wasn't paying attention got hurt, or worse.

"I think I see Jess," Maya called over her shoulder. She released my hand and took off toward her boyfriend. He was what Maya called a gym bear—or was it a muscled bear—whatever that was. He was certainly burly. And big. And muscled.

Normally, I never judged my best friend's choices in men. But I wished she'd stick to one for longer than the time period we had to pay our rent each month.

Echoes of cheers and guffaws bounced off the walls as we neared a large, square doorway. From the volume of noise, there had to be double the spectators by the arena. I wanted to cover my ears, but I was too stunned at what we'd stepped onto.

We were on a walkway that lined the perimeter of this gargantuan space.

No sooner had Maya left my side, then the congestion of human bodies in the doorway pushed forward and I was mashed up against the black metal railing, my body bowing slightly forward. An overwhelming queasiness settled in my stomach as I stared at the lower half of the warehouse.

My head spun from the drastic height. Between the bloody faces of the fighters in the large octagonal cage and the rising screams from the blood thirsty people crowding the arena, I needed to get the hell out of there. But I was wedged tight to the railing, and I couldn't escape.

And since falling from the second floor of this building wasn't how I wanted to die, I quickly seized the moment when the crowd of onlookers disbursed down the gangplank that led to the lower level. I squeezed past the enthralled observers that remained, and plastered myself to the wall, taking deep breaths until my heart wasn't thrashing against my ribs.

I contemplated if I should just leave, but Maya shouted my name over the roaring crowd.

"Regi."

I glared at her, silently conveying that *This is far from fun.*

She gave me one of her smirks, then her eyes shifted to the left. I followed her gaze and my annoyance grew into utter frustration. The last person I wanted to see was standing next to Jess.

Kane Maxwell. He was one of Jess's friends. Three weeks ago, Maya dragged me to his penthouse, where he'd thrown a lavish party. Want to talk about pretentious?

Kane obviously thought highly of himself, because he'd made it extremely clear that all he wanted out of me that night was a fuck, and I could be one of the lucky ones to have his dick down my throat.

To his surprise, I had told him to drop his dick down somewhere else, and left the party. But apparently, given the wide, evil grin currently pasted on his somewhat handsome face, Kane hadn't gotten the hint I wasn't interested.

If I was any other desperate woman, I would have

taken him up on his offer to ride him like a champion bull —his words, not mine. But I wasn't that kind of girl. Besides, he set off the creeper alert. And I'd learned a long time ago to follow my instincts with guys like him.

"Regina, I'm so glad you came," Kane said as I approached with caution. Gah, I hated when he used my full name.

He was about to reach for me, but I halted, just out of range of his beefy fingers.

"Hi, Kane," I replied evenly, but my narrowed eyes were on my best friend who was fake smiling at me like I was wrong. But Maya knew better.

I gave her the *You're in trouble* glare. She gave back her, *I didn't know he was going to be here* eyes. I returned her stare with *You're a liar*.

"Since we're all here, how about we head down to the main floor and take our seats. The next fight will start in ten minutes," Jess suggested, before he wrapped a brawny arm around Maya and planted a hard, quick kiss to her mouth.

"Great idea. Can we get a drink first, babe?" Maya bounced with exuberance.

"You ladies can have whatever you want. It's on the house," Kane said and winked at me.

On the house? Gah. Is he for real?

I wasn't going to ask what he meant by that. Instead, I followed the three of them down to the main floor. We got the drinks at the bar, then headed to a set of seats in the front row, where the view of the fight was unobstructed.

We were so close that I could see the blood splatters on the edges of the gray mat in the cage.

Maya squealed in delight at how close we were. Me, on the other hand... I wanted to get out of there.

I swallowed the bit of bile in the back of my throat from the brutality of the fight that was taking place, and washed it down with some of my southern comfort and soda. I welcomed the burn.

We sat boy-girl, and, for some unlucky reason, I got stuck between Jess and Kane. I wanted to tell Kane to move over since he was practically glued to my side. However, during the two minutes we were sitting there, he scooched even closer and then Jess did the same. I was literally sandwiched tight between the hulking men and wanted to rail at them to move. But for Maya's sake, I clamped my mouth shut, kept my eyes straight ahead, and sipped the rest of my drink slowly.

I wasn't a person that got off on watching two people fighting for money—I didn't find it the least bit titillating. Actually, it turned me the fuck off.

Nevertheless, I hadn't known Maya was so blood-thirsty, until she was cheering for the fighters to beat the hell out of each other.

I couldn't watch this, or her. "Where's the bathroom?" I asked Kane.

He pointed to the far side of the wall where we'd walked in from. I gave him a nod and got up, but Kane stood with me.

"I can go to the bathroom by myself, Kane," I said with barely there civility.

"This is a dangerous place for a single woman to walk alone. Appease me, sweetheart," Kane said with sugar lacing his tone. Like that was going to make me cow to his whims. *Not.*

"I'm not your sweetheart. And I can take care of myself." I didn't wait for his reply and stalked off toward the bathroom. Luckily, Kane didn't follow me.

The bathroom was bare bones, with two stalls and a single sink. But it had the privacy I needed.

At least there's toilet paper.

I took my time and did my business, absorbing the semi-quiet of the concrete space. The thick walls dampened the shouts and yells from the crowd. I then washed my hands and walked back, dreading the entire way.

However, Kane wasn't even there when I returned to our seats. In fact, Jess wasn't either. With a quick glance at the cage, relief washed over me that the fight was over.

I dropped next to Maya and scowled at my friend. "I'm leaving. Are you going to coming with me or not?" I posed.

Maya opened her mouth, but she was cut off by the announcer booming over the intercom. We both swiveled toward the direction of the cage and I immediately spotted Kane and Jess, with a huge, muscled guy in black shorts and a short white robe, throwing small jabs in the air.

Before I could ask Maya again if she wanted to leave, the cage announcer spoke.

"All eyes to me, ladies and gentlemen," he said, and patiently waited for the noise to die down. "We have a special treat for you tonight. First to walk into the cage is none other than Forest Sulley, the current middleweight champion of the UGF tournaments. With six consecutive knockouts, two first round knockout wins, and a total of twelve straight wins."

The roar of the crowd was deafening. Maya was bouncing in her seat while I put my hands over my ears until the noise ceased, and my eyes darted from my friend to the announcer.

"His competitor is no stranger to the world of fighting. With seven knockouts, five first round wins, and a total of twenty-one wins under his belt, let's welcome middleweight champion, Krew Mathews."

My entire body locked up at the name the cage announcer had spoken. *Krew.*

That wasn't a typical name for parents to pick for their child.

"No. That can't be," I whispered and immediately stood. My eyes shifted around the interior of the cage, but I didn't see the other fighter.

Then I caught sight of a tall, not-so-lean fighter, striding toward the arena. He had on a black robe, with the hood up. I couldn't see his face to determine if that was Krew. My Krew.

"Regi." I heard Maya calling my name, but I was so focused on seeing this other fighter's face that I didn't realize I was at the cage, my fingers clamped onto the black fencing and my face mere inches from the links.

The loud thrashing of my heart drowned out all the cacophonies of hoots and hollers around me. With the rising anticipation of seeing this fighter's face, I held my breath. I wanted to deny it was Krew Gatlin, the boy I fell for—the boy and that life I ran from was here.

Life couldn't be that cruel.

It had been thirteen years since I had last seen his handsome face and those golden amber eyes. But seeing Krew now—in that ring—was the last place I wanted him to be.

"What are you doing, Regi? You can't stand here." Maya yanked me back, but I refused and pushed her hands off me. I wasn't going to move, not until I saw that man's face. I had to be sure it was *my* Krew.

The hood slipped back from the fighter's head and exposed that familiar face. My stomach bottomed out, and so did my feet. Then our eyes locked onto each other through the fence links, and shock froze his features.

Tears of the past were reborn. Anger, heartbreak, and fear slid in as the memory of those last few days I had with Krew and Decker filled my head, before our lives imploded.

As Krew turned his head away and refocused on the other fighter, I couldn't catch my breath. The whirlwind of emotions clogged my throat, and I stood there as my lungs demanded more oxygen.

Maya had a death grip on my arm, and I let her pull me away from the cage.

She was talking to me, but I couldn't hear a word she was saying as we took our seats.

"Regi?" Maya cupped my face with her free hand.

I swiped the tears away and uttered, "That's my Krew up there."

Maya glanced up at the arena. "I know," she whispered in face. "I'm just as shocked as you are."

But was she really? I thought she had seen the line-up of fighters earlier? She was talking about a few of them on the drive here.

I turned back to get another look at the man I had missed so much, and my entire being turned to ice. Another set of memories poured in like acid, and my mind scrambled to find the words that clogged my throat. "I—I have to go."

"Regi—" Maya cast another glance to the cage and frowned deeply. "Go," she urged, but never looked away from the one person who had changed my world to black.

I didn't respond as I tore out of her arms with only one thought in mind.

Run.